UNCLE VAMPIRE

Books by
CYNTHIA D. GRANT

Phoenix Rising
Keep Laughing
Shadow Man
Uncle Vampire

UNCLE VAMPIRE

CYNTHIA D. GRANT

Atheneum Books for Young Readers

Atheneum Books for Young Readers
An imprint of Simon & Schuster Children's Publishing Division
1230 Avenue of the Americas
New York, New York 10020

First edition
Printed in the United States of America
10 9 8 7 6 5 4 3 2

Library of Congress Cataloging-in-Publication Data

Grant, Cynthia D.
Uncle Vampire / C.D. Grant.—1st ed.
p.   cm.
Summary: Sixteen-year-old Caroline and her twin sister Honey know
for sure that their Uncle Toddy is a vampire who comes at night to
drink their blood, but fear of the consequences makes them keep their
terrible secret.
ISBN 0-689-31852-9
[1. Incest—Fiction.   2. Family problems—Fiction.   3. Emotional
problems—Fiction.]   I. Title.
PZ7.G76672Un   1993
[Fic]—dc20   92-44455

THIS ONE'S FOR YOU, REGAN,
AND FOR GAIL PARIS,
AND FOR THE MEMBERS OF
THE PRINCESS OF POWER CLUB.
MAY THEIR TIARAS TWINKLE ALL ACROSS THE LAND.

They've always liked her better than me. I don't blame them. She's sweet. My parents call her Honey. They always call me by my name.

We're close. Twins. Mirror images. We can almost read each other's minds. Usually that's fine, but it can be a pain. A family can become too ingrown; interwoven thistles, inseparable, brittle.

That's what happens when there's a secret at the core.

Sometimes the secret prickles at the corners of her mind, but Honey wipes it away; she wants to be happy. She wants to have a perfect life.

"You can't pretend it's not happening," I'll say.

"What's not happening?" She'll play dumb. Lately that fills me with rage.

You have to face facts, accept reality. Acknowledge some solid truths. Then maybe things will start to get better. But Honey says, "No, look at these flowers. Listen to this pretty music. Let's not think about ugly things. What's the point in being depressed?"

We've gone over this a million times. In the past, we always agreed. No more.

We got into another hassle today. We were upstairs, in our bedroom.

I said, "I don't see why we can't have the big room." Our older sister Margaret's room, down the hall.

1

"Uncle Toddy's got it. It's full of his stuff."

Maggie is away at college. The folks think she'll move back someday. I doubt it. She didn't even come home to visit last summer. She said she had to work. Sometimes I feel like I'll die if I can't see Maggie. She's three thousand miles away, in Boston.

"Richie gets a big room."

"He's a boy," Honey said, as if that explained everything. Richie's supposed to graduate from high school this year. At the moment, he's flunking out.

"Why can't he sleep in the den downstairs?"

"Because Papa works in there!"

He used to have an office downtown, but he couldn't afford the rent. He sells insurance. Not enough of it, apparently.

I said, "Why don't they kick Uncle Toddy out?"

"He doesn't have a job! He has no place to live! Why do we have to talk about this again?"

"The man is a vampire," I pointed out.

The word always makes Honey flinch.

"Don't say that."

"You know it's true."

"He can't help it."

"Oh, please, don't make excuses for him!" She is such an apologist.

"Anyway, he's not hurting you—"

"I can't believe you'd say that! Are you completely crazy?" I paced around the room.

"It's not like he kills people," Honey said.

"No, he just drinks their blood. What a break."

"It hardly ever happens. Just when he can't help it."
Honey rearranged the stuffed animals on her bed. "Be
sure to wear your cross. It might keep him away."

"I wear it all the time! It doesn't help." My cross was
on a gold chain beneath my blouse. I yanked it out and
waved it in her face. "Why do you have to pretend it's
not happening?"

"Because it's not a big deal! It isn't something I can
change. Why can't you forget about it and be happy?"
Honey brushed the honey-colored hair that pours thick
and soft to her waist. "Lots of things are fine. Mama's
good lately." Honey dusted the top of her immaculate
bureau, then the desk and the armchair by the window.
Our room is so neat it looks vacant.

"Sure," I said, "she's fine, unless you tell her something she doesn't want to hear. Then she gets that look
on her face, like: Please don't tell me that or I'll go
crazy. Richie's so unhappy lately."

"He's going through a phase."

"Acting like a zombie is a phase?"

"He's not a zombie. You exaggerate everything. Why
can't you just be happy?"

She's a cheerleader, for God's sake. Imagine how
that makes me feel, watching her jerk around like a
puppet in front of a crowd of strangers. She says:
There's nothing wrong with being proud of my school.

Why do you have to cut everything down? Don't come to the games, if you don't want to.

"I guess I'm not trying hard enough," I said.

"I won't talk to you, if you're going to be sarcastic," Honey said, and left the room.

She does that sometimes; walks out, disappears somewhere in the house, and ignores me for a while. Then she gets over it. We don't like to fight. Divided we don't stand a chance.

Maybe, like she says, I'm overreacting. Imagining things. Being dramatic. Vampires can be perfectly nice. They don't stand out in a crowd; they hide their fangs. Uncle Toddy appears completely normal. His face looks young until you get up close and see all the little lines. Then you realize, with a shock: He's not eighteen. Uncle Toddy is thirty-five.

He can't seem to keep a job. This has gone on for years. Something always happens and it's not his fault. People are jealous of him because he's so good-looking. Or he's smarter than the boss, so he gets fired. Then he has to give up his apartment and move back here. He's Papa's baby brother.

Uncle Toddy never acts like a vampire around my folks, so Honey and I figure they don't know. Or don't want to know, so they tell themselves they don't. Like the time the skunks moved under the porch, and we didn't know how to make them go away so we all pretended we couldn't smell them. Tuning out reality is a consuming family passion. It gobbles up everyone's attention. If I set my bangs on fire at the dinner table, Mama would ask me if I'd lightened my hair.

Honey and I think Richie knows about our uncle, even though Uncle Toddy leaves him alone. Richie's sad because he knows that our uncle is a vampire and there isn't anything he can do about it. So now he hardly talks at all. He's gone down deep inside of himself and won't come out anymore. I miss him.

Honey was back and fiddling with her hair in front of the mirror on the closet door. She said, "Why do you make things sound worse than they are?"

"Why do you make them sound better?"

"You just like to argue."

"Our uncle is a vampire! He could be terrorizing the neighborhood, for all we know."

"He's not."

"You don't know that!"

"Listen to me," Honey said, deliberately, as if she were talking to an idiot. "There's nothing we can do. He doesn't have any money. When he's working again, he'll move out."

"When hell freezes over, he'll sell snow cones," I said.

Honey didn't get mad. She knew I was sad.

"Don't worry. Everything is going to be fine. God wouldn't let anything bad happen to us."

"It's already happening. Where's God?"

"Everywhere." Honey touched the gold cross at her throat. She does that all the time.

I said, "Maybe the folks are vampires too. Maybe we're zombies and we don't even know it. The living dead, condemned to roam the earth in search of human blood."

"Don't be disgusting."

"Anything's possible in this big, wide, wonderful world!"

"Sarcasm is never attractive."

"Yes, Mama. Yes, Papa."

"You're impossible." Honey threw down her brush. "No wonder everybody thinks you're a pain."

"Ouch! Down and dirty! Honey gets funky!"

"Now I really am leaving."

"You can't escape me! I'll haunt you from the grave!"

"You've been watching too many movies." She left.

It's true. Watching movies, especially old ones from the forties and fifties, is one of my favorite things to do. They're black and white. No lurid colors. They've got a beginning, a middle, and an end. The story starts, the plot develops; the people solve the mystery, or get married, or killed. Whatever. Something *happens*. Then it's over. And it makes sense.

Around here, nothing makes sense, or ends. We're trapped in the middle forever.

Now Honey's playing the piano. When in doubt, practice. Loud. She fills up her head with classical stuff.

Too bad it's not a pipe organ. All we're missing around here is some spooky music.

Uncle Toddy appears to tell me dinner's ready. He's smiling. My friends think he's handsome and cute. Mostly I notice his teeth.

"How's it going?" he says.

"Fine."

We never talk to him about being a vampire. It's a difficult subject to discuss, to work into polite conversation. Politeness is everything. Don't rock the boat. Don't make waves. You might drown. But I think the time has come to confront him, to tell the police or our minister or someone. Honey says no; he'd get in trouble, and anyway, no one would believe us. Everybody knows that vampires are a myth and exist only in our imagination.

"Come and eat now, Carolyn." He pats my shoulder.

"Okay," I say. "I'll be right there."

I keep my eyes empty so he can't see inside me. My eyes are mirrors, reflecting Uncle Toddy's smiling face.

The trouble with secrets is that they're
so inconvenient. You have to keep
covering them up all the time. You'd
think we'd be used to that by now.
But covering up is getting harder.

When we were little, friends
played at our house. There's a rusty
swing set in our big backyard. The slide lies on the
ground.

We had lemonade stands and belonged to the
Brownies. My mother led a troop for a while. Things
started to change. . . . I am trying to remember when.
It's hard. There are so many closed doors to the past,
just like there are in our house.

Things began to change when Uncle Toddy came to
live here. At first his visits were lots of fun; he was full
of laughter and surprises and games. Like us, he was
young. He wanted to be a policeman when he grew up.
Or a fireman, a good guy. That didn't work out. He
joined the navy for a while. Then he came back, he
always came back, and the den downstairs filled up
with his stuff. Once we found a magazine on his bed,
full of pictures of naked women. The ladies were pretty,
although their faces looked strange—pained or pout-
ing. Margaret said men like those magazines, even our
father. She'd seen a lot of *Playboy*s when she baby-sat
at different houses.

Maggie was a good big sister. She was never mean

to us kids. We'd go into her room when she was out and listen to her radio and try on her boots. She always knew when we'd been in there, even though we left no clues. She was smart.

The older Maggie got, the more she was gone: baby-sitting, working, studying at the library. It seemed like she was never home. Meanwhile, Uncle Toddy became a permanent guest. "He's my brother! I can't throw him out!" Papa said. He and Mama argued about him sometimes. Uncle Toddy knew Mama didn't want him to live there, so he brought her pots of African violets and helped with the housework and cooking. Those had never been Mama's favorite chores. After a while she liked having him around. He made bookcases and birdhouses in his shop in the cellar. His occasional jobs were usually on the graveyard shift. "I'm a night owl," he explained.

He was a wonderful help when Mama had her break-down. That was many years ago, but I can't forget it. She was screaming and scared and not making any sense. All the kids in the neighborhood (in the world, it seemed) were standing on the sidewalk in front of our house when she left in the ambulance. The kids hung around out there for hours, waiting for something more to happen, for somebody else to go crazy.

Papa says there's nothing wrong with Mama. She just has a delicate disposition. Treat her gently. If we're having problems at school, for instance, we're supposed to tell him or Uncle Toddy. The trouble is, my father's gone a lot, trying to scare up business. When he's here he doesn't want to be bothered. He holds that newspaper in front of his face like a shield, preferring the world's bad news to ours.

The other day I tried to talk to him about Richie. Things aren't going well for him at school, I said. My father looked peeved, as if Richie were having problems just to get attention.

"The trouble with Richie is, he's selfish," my father said. "He's always been that way. He never thinks of anyone but himself."

That's not true. My brother was a happy boy. He loved to sing and to give people things, flowers he'd picked, or dimes for my bank. He extravagantly praised my crayoned drawings. "A purple horse! That's wonderful, Carolyn."

He's different now. It's hard to tell what he's thinking. He won't say, and I can't read his face. When I ask him what's wrong, he says, "Nothing's wrong." He never does his homework and cuts school a lot. It will be a miracle if he graduates. It's as if he doesn't care anymore. About himself. About anything.

A couple of his teachers have stopped me in the halls and said, "What's wrong with Richie?" And I say, "Nothing's wrong." Then I wonder which is betrayal: lies or truth.

I wish I could talk to Maggie about this. I've left

messages on her phone machine. It's hard to get hold of her; she's always at school or working. It's three hours later there. That bothers me. I wish we were in the same time zone. The last time she called, we couldn't really talk; everybody was hanging around the phone, wanting to talk to her too.

I started a letter to her but never finished it. Then it got lost. Anyway, it sounded too spacey: Uncle Toddy's a vampire. Did you know that, Maggie? He's draining me. He's sucking all the life out of this house. Richie's strange. He never talks. He used to be happy. Now he's not. He hasn't been happy for a long, long time. I kept noticing he'd changed, but then I'd forget. I feel like I'm sleep-walking through my life. Occasionally I wake up and look around, but my eyes want to close; they don't like what they see. Mama stays in her room and reads and reads. She prefers books to life, which she doesn't like and which can't be returned to the library. Papa's business is doing poorly. I think he invested and lost a lot of money. Besides all that, Maggie, everything's fine!

Nobody wants to read a letter like that. Or write one.

It's easier for me to face things than it is for Honey. She tries so hard to have a normal life, getting good grades, being a cheerleader. Yea, team! She won't let people come to our house. "It's easier to meet them someplace else," she says. Sometimes when our uncle looks at our friends, his eyes almost glaze with greed.

We meet our friends at the library downtown, or we

wait out in front when they come to pick us up, to go
to the movies or to parties or to games.

"Invite your friends in," Uncle Toddy always says.

"They're in a hurry," we say, flying out the front
door.

He especially likes my best friend, Nancy. She's
known him since she was little. He still calls her Freckle
Face. She dropped by recently. I found them laughing
in the kitchen. She thinks he's handsome and very cool,
unlike most adults.

He's not like most adults at all.

I dragged her out of the house. "Come on. We're
late."

"What's the rush?" she said when we got to the
porch. "The library doesn't close for hours. You act like
you're ashamed of your house."

There's nothing wrong with the house. It could use
some paint, but it's a nice big place, a handsome house.
And we are a handsome family. We had a family picture
taken at church last month. Mama bought a silver frame
for it and put it on the piano. We're clustered in a
smiling group: Grammy, Grampa, Mama, Papa, Honey,
Uncle Vampire . . .

I try not to see him that way, but I can't help it.
We'll be sitting around the table, having dinner or
celebrating somebody's birthday, and I see him as if I
had X-ray vision—the cave of his mouth, the teeth, the
claws.

Does he tell me he wants to drink my blood?

No. He says, "Pass the potatoes, please, Carolyn."

Honey doesn't see Uncle Toddy as I do. She shuts that picture out of her mind. "He's our uncle, he loves us," Honey tells me. I wish I had her faith.

Sometimes when we're all at church (except for Uncle Toddy and Richie; Richie won't come anymore), I ask God: What did we do to deserve this? Why did you give us this cross to bear? God, you who have the power to raise mountains, part the seas, destroy cities—why won't you make one vampire uncle disappear?

Honey says that's selfish. She says God has so many people coming to him with problems, terrible problems, much worse than ours, that he can't grant every little wish. Besides, she says, God never gives people more trouble than they can endure. My grandma says that too. She believes in God, and I believe in Grammy. She always loves me, no matter what I do. She used to make me feel so safe. Now she's old. I sit beside her in the pew. I help her stand up when it's time to sing a hymn.

Lately I feel like the weight is too great. My family is a huge stone on my chest. I gasp for breath (am I dreaming or awake?) and Mama's eyes are on me: "Are you all right, Carolyn?"

"It's so hot in here," I whisper back.

The church is filled. It's a large congregation. When I was there I used to feel like nothing could ever hurt me. There were so many of us we could march out of the church and into the streets and crush all the sin and sorrow in the world. Jesus is my savior. He is always beside me. No matter what happens, I am never alone. Jesus watches over me. That's what Grammy tells me, and I love her so much that it must be true.

When darkness reaches for me and plucks me from sleep and carries me out the window on his billowing black wings, I am never alone. God is with me. I pray silently so that the monster cannot hear me. Our Father, who art in heaven, hallowed be Thy name. Thy kingdom come, Thy will be done (*the monster's breath scorches my eyelids, my skin*) on earth as it is in heaven. Give us this day our daily bread, and forgive us our trespasses as we forgive those (*how can I, Lord?*) who trespass against us. Lead us not into temptation, but deliver us from evil (*deliver me, Lord! I'm dying*). For Thine is the kingdom, the power, and the glory. Forever and ever. Amen.

Uncle Toddy doesn't show his fangs during the day. Vampires fear the light. He's a night person. That's when he goes out on dates. We never meet the women he's seeing. He just got another job, on the night shift, of course. He says he's a security guard. I don't believe him.

Forgive me, God, I have even thought of killing him. Of plunging a knife into his heart. But I don't have the power. I am growing weak. I pray to God for strength to endure. In a couple of years I'll be able to leave, like Margaret did. Why doesn't she come back? Does she know he's a vampire? If she knew, she would never abandon me. She and my father didn't get along. They argued, about politics and what she should do. She couldn't wait to leave for college.

I'm trying to hold on until I can escape, but I feel like I'm going to shatter. It didn't used to be so hard to be happy. Like Honey, I turned my eyes toward the light. Now the darkness is all around me.

Sometimes I think: Maybe it's me. Maybe I'm crazy and imagining everything. My parents always tell me I'm an actress; that I invent drama to keep life interesting. How on earth could my uncle be a vampire? Vampires are a myth based on a man who lived in the Middle Ages, a cruel prince known as Vlad the Impaler, who tortured peasants and drank their blood.

But Honey's seen him too; she's smelled his breath. She doesn't want to talk about that anymore. The last time I tried, she drowned me out with the piano. Other times she runs away.

That drives me mad because we've got to face this. Maybe if we told our parents, they'd call the police, they'd throw him out. Honey says no, we can't tell them. She says they've got enough on their minds without some stupid fantasy.

She's not being honest, with herself or me. I think

she's afraid that if we tell Mama and Papa that Uncle Toddy is a vampire, they'll look at us with flat zombie eyes and say, "So what? Shut up."

That would kill Honey. She'd rather live in a dream where they care about us than wake up and find out they don't.

I don't know how much longer I can stand this. I feel like I'm buried alive. My heart is thrashing and my lungs are bulging, trying to find breath in this airless house.

At dinner tonight, Mama says to me: "You're awfully quiet."

All around the table, eyes fasten on my face. Even Richie is looking. Honey nudges me; she doesn't want trouble.

I pretend to be too busy chewing to answer.

My father says, "Carolyn, don't sit there staring at your mother. Answer her."

I swallow. "I'm fine," I say. And smile.

My father says, "That's my girl."

Honey and I talked while we walked to school this morning. We decided that Uncle Toddy can't be a vampire. That must have been a bad dream we had.

Honey ticked off the facts on her manicured fingers. "He doesn't look like a vampire. He doesn't sleep in a coffin. He's really nice. He packs our lunch every morning. Think about it."

"How could we have had the same dream?" I asked.

"You had it first and told me about it. I got all freaked out and had it too. Now we're all worked up for nothing."

"It doesn't feel like nothing," I said.

But it's hard to believe in vampires when the sun is shining and little kids stream down the sidewalks on their way to school. Cars drive by, people heading toward their jobs, and you can hear the flag snapping above the school, a brisk flap like a slap across the face. *Wake up, you were having a nightmare, but it's over now. It's morning.*

"The problem is you're not getting enough sleep," Honey said. "You stay up too late, reading."

I hate to turn off the light. Vampires come out at night. I lie in the dark, my eyes wide open, listening to every creak in that house. So I read and read, my eyes burning. Asleep, I'm as defenseless as a baby.

"Take some vitamins. Take care of yourself. You're getting too skinny," Honey said.

"Look who's talking."

"I'm supposed to be skinny. Cheerleaders can't be fat."

Honey's very vain about her looks and it's no wonder; people are fools for pretty girls with blue eyes and long blond hair. In ninth grade she was voted Most Popular and Best Smile. I think people voted for her hair. We have lots of friends at school, we've known them forever. They don't think it's weird that we don't invite them home; adults are there. We tend to meet at homes where the parents are away, working. Not that we drink or smoke or get high; our friends aren't like that. We just talk and laugh and hang around. There hasn't been much time for that lately. Honey's busy with school and piano lessons and cheerleading, and I have a lead in the winter play, portraying Laura in *The Glass Menagerie*. Mrs. Bennett, the play's director and my English teacher, says I'm doing a terrific job of capturing Laura's fragile, childlike qualities.

I memorized my lines right away, but at the last rehearsal I couldn't keep them straight. I was saying the wrong thing at the wrong time. School used to feel so separate and safe, but now I'm always worrying about my family. They leak into everything I do. Last night I heard Papa and Uncle Toddy arguing about money. Uncle Toddy said security guard jobs don't pay much and he was giving Papa every cent he could toward rent and food. A lot of Uncle Toddy's money goes into his truck. It's fixed up as cheery as the pickups belonging to the high school boys who cruise by our house, hoping to catch a glimpse of Honey.

"Look, there's Richie!" Honey waved as he flew by on his motorcycle. He didn't see us. He wasn't wearing his helmet, or heading toward school. "He's probably getting one of his friends," she added.

"He's probably cutting class."

"You don't know that. Why are you always so negative?"

"I wish Margaret would come home," I said.

"It's her last year of college. She's got her own life now. Maybe she'll come home for Christmas."

"I doubt it."

"Will you look on the bright side for a change?" Honey put a smile on her face as we walked into the school.

I have English first period. I like Mrs. Bennett. She tells me I'm a good writer, that I have imagination and talent. Nancy's in that class. She passed me a note that read: "I need to talk to you at lunch. I've got incredible news." She could've leaned across the aisle and told me, but notes are much more fun.

After English I have history, geometry, and PE.

School has always been easy for me and Honey. I plan to go to college. I'd like to be a journalist and maybe write some fiction. Papa says that's a lousy way to make money. Honey wants to be a model or a flight attendant. She's all hopped up about traveling around the world for free. Papa thinks that's a great idea; college is expensive.

I rode on a plane once, to Papa's mother's funeral. It scared me, being way up in the air. How does a heavy plane stay up there? I can't figure out how that works. Honey says: "Who cares how it works? It does! You don't know how a car works either, but you want to learn to drive one, don't you?"

Yes and no. I guess I should. Cars scare me too. They're heavy and fast, crowding all around you, so close. The only thing that keeps you from being smashed any second is those little white lines on the road.

Honey says I worry too much. She's right. I wish I could turn off worry, like she does. I wish I could be happy all the time.

Nancy and I had lunch at the pizza place, which was packed with kids from school. They crowded around our table. Nancy's popular too. Rolling her eyes hugely, she finally said, "Do you mind? We're trying to have a private conversation!" Everybody laughed and gave us space.

Nancy looks almost exactly like she did in third grade, except for her body, which has changed.

"Guess what!" She lowered her voice dramatically. "Guess who asked me to the winter dance!"

"Bobby Sloane," I said. "Do I win a prize?" He's a nice guy, a football player.

She pretended to pout. "I wanted to surprise you!"

"How could I be surprised? Once you decided he was taking you, he didn't stand a chance."

"But isn't it wonderful? I'm so happy! Maybe we can all go together."

"I don't know if I'll go," I said. I'd declined several invitations. This wasn't a good time to ask my folks to spend money on a fancy dress.

"You have to go! You're such a dud. What's the matter with you?"

"I'm tired, I guess."

"So take a nap! The dance is weeks away."

"I'm pretty busy with school and the play."

"Oh, baloney." Nancy's always called a spade a spade. "What's wrong with you? You seem so different lately."

"I've got a lot on my mind."

"Like what? You can tell me." Nancy's brown eyes warmed with concern. Many times I've almost told her that my uncle is a vampire. But I chicken out. She likes him. Nancy would think I'm crazy.

Besides, he told me not to tell. In the dream I had.

That Honey dreamed too. He warned us. The words float away, out of reach. What did he say? I can't remember.

"I don't know what's wrong," I said. My millionth lie, a new world's record. "I just feel weird."

"Is your mother okay?"

"She's doing all right. My father—his business isn't doing too well."

That sliver of truth made me cringe with guilt. Money is one of our family secrets. We look like we have a lot more than we do. Papa just bought a new car, to impress his clients. The clients he hopes to attract with his success.

"That's scary," Nancy said. She knows about money problems. Her parents owned a restaurant that closed. Now they're running a smaller place.

"It's not just that." I was struggling to be honest. I used to tell Nancy everything. But over the years . . . I've screened things from her. Things I don't want to hear myself say.

"It's Richie," I said. "He's flunking out. He looks so bad. Real pale and spacey—"

"I know," Nancy said. "It's really sad. What do your parents say?"

"They don't even notice! It's like they go around with bags over their heads! He comes down for dinner and doesn't say a word—for weeks! But do they ask him if anything's wrong? No! If they did, he might tell them, and they don't want to hear it. It's disgusting. It makes me so mad."

Nancy patted my arm with her freckled hand. "Have you talked to Richie? He might listen to you."

"We're not close anymore. He's pulled away."

"That's what happens when people take drugs. They change."

"Drugs?" I said. "What do you mean, drugs?"

"Downers. Tranks. I thought you knew."

"Tranks?" I plunged into a bottomless shaft. Nancy's voice was far away.

"Tranquilizers. Even the teachers know."

Nancy wouldn't lie to me. I gaped in her face. "Are you sure?"

"That's what everybody says. Why don't you ask him?" Nancy squeezed my hand. "I'm sorry, Carolyn. I thought you knew what was happening."

"I thought so too. I thought he was depressed."

I couldn't finish my lunch. We went back to class. The afternoon passed in a haze; teachers talking, pencils scratching, papers being shuffled and collected.

After school I walked home alone. Uncle Toddy was watching a TV talk show.

"How was school, sweetie?"

"Fine. Where's Mama?"

"Lying down," he said. "What do you need?"

"Nothing." I started up the stairs.

"We're having lasagna tonight, your favorite," he called.

I went into Richie's bedroom and shut the door. It looked like someone had been murdered in there. Clothes and books and shoes were everywhere. Cassette tapes littered his unmade bed.

I tore apart his room. He wouldn't notice the difference. I searched for something that wasn't there—a bottle of poison bearing a skull and crossbones. I found only empty cigarette packages.

I went into my room and lay down on my bed. The shadows from the bare tree outside my window splayed cracks across the ceiling. I heard Uncle Toddy moving around in the kitchen.

Maybe I could talk to Grammy about Richie. She only lives a mile away. I could curl up on her bed, as I had when I was little, and she would cuddle me and tell funny stories. Being in her house always made me feel safe.

Now she's old. She and Grampa are frail. It scares me to notice them changing. I can't talk to her about Richie. She wouldn't understand. Drugs? Our Richie? He's such a good boy. . . . Grammy's eyes would fill with tears, and I would be to blame.

Once, years ago, I tried to tell her about Uncle Toddy. I'd told Papa, but he said I was pretending. He got mad. So I tried to tell Grammy. How old was I?

Little. My plaid school dress. A fragment of memory. My plaid school dress with the lacy white collar. I loved that dress. I thought I looked pretty. I didn't know about vampires. I couldn't find the right words. I only knew that his yellow eyes scared me and that his smile was a big red hole.

We were in her cozy kitchen. She was making me cinnamon toast, cut into squares the way I liked it.

I leaned against her side so I could feel her warmth.

"Uncle Toddy's scary," I told her.

"Scary? No, Uncle Toddy's not scary. You just don't know him very well," she said.

"I don't like him, Grammy."

She frowned at me. I hardly ever saw a frown on my Grammy's face. "You mustn't say that, Carolyn. He's your daddy's brother. Uncle Toddy is your uncle. He loves you."

Her disapproval shamed me. I was always her favorite. I couldn't bear to have her pull away. "I'm sorry, Grammy." She reached down and hugged me. I smiled and ate my toast.

When I came down for dinner, Uncle Toddy said, "How's the play coming along, Carolyn?"

I hadn't gone to the rehearsal. I'd forgotten all about it. Something was wrong with my mind.

"The rehearsal was canceled. Mrs. Bennett was sick," I said. Lying gets easier all the time.

I thought the alarm clock had woken me up, but it was Honey. She was sobbing.

"What's the matter? Is he here?" I was instantly alert. I reached under the pillow for my new knife. Its four-inch blade is shiny and sharp. I bought it with my baby-sitting money.

Honey wouldn't stop crying.

"Quit it. You're going to wake up the whole house," I said. It was two o'clock in the morning.

Our bedroom door opened. Uncle Toddy stood in the doorway, the hall light behind him, his face in shadow.

"Carolyn, are you all right?" he asked. "Honey, are you okay?"

"Everything's fine," I said.

"I was dreaming," Honey added.

"It sounded like somebody was crying." Tears are one of his favorite drinks.

The hand holding the knife crept under the blankets, where Uncle Toddy couldn't see it.

"I was having a bad dream. I'm okay now," Honey said.

"Is anything wrong? Would you like to talk?"

"No thanks. I'm sleepy." She faked a yawn. "I'm sorry I woke you up."

That pissed me off. Why does she always apologize? That bastard haunts our dreams.

Uncle Toddy felt the wall for the overhead light switch.

"Get out. Don't turn that on," I said. His eyes would've feasted on her swollen face.

"What's the matter with you, Carolyn? Are you sure you're awake?"

"Wide awake. I'm never going to close my eyes again."

"Lower your voice. Your parents are sleeping."

"They're always sleeping! They're in a trance." But I could sense them downstairs, frozen, listening. Honey was pretending to be asleep again, but I knew she was listening too.

It was too dark to see my uncle's expression, but I know how he looks when he's angry. His smile mask slides off, baring his face, revealing his true identity.

He stepped into the room and clenched his fists.

"What's the matter with you lately? You're acting so strange. You're doing too much stuff after school. We hardly ever see you. You're never home."

"Gee, and this is such a fun place!"

"You're losing it, Carolyn. Better pull yourself together."

"Do you think I'm stupid? Do you think I'm insane? Do you think I don't know what's going on?" I pulled my gold cross out of my nightgown, but it didn't drive him back. Like me, it's too small.

"Carolyn," he whispered, "shall I call the ambulance? Do you need professional help? Is that it? Do you want to go away, like your mother did?"

That woke Honey up. "I'm not crazy!" she cried.

Uncle Vampire turned tender. Our tears make him soft. He loves the salty taste of sorrow.

"Of course you're not crazy, Honey. You were having a bad dream," he murmured. "You've been under so much pressure at school. They expect too much from you kids. It's not right."

"You're the one who's driving everybody crazy!" I said.

He sighed and shook his head. "Carolyn, you're not making any sense at all. I'm really worried about you."

But his words weren't directed at me; we had an audience. Richie had materialized behind my uncle. His eyes were wide with alarm.

"What's the matter?" he said. "What's going on?"

"Nothing," Honey said. "I was having a bad dream. I'm sorry I woke everybody up."

"Are you sure you're all right?"

"Everything's under control now, Rich," Uncle Toddy said. "Go back to bed."

"You know, don't you, Richie? He's a vampire," I said.

Honey cringed, rocking back and forth. "He's a vampire, Richie. He's drinking our blood. He's killing the whole family!"

The lamp in the hallway lit my brother's face. The horror in his eyes was like a knife through my tongue. He looked at me as if I were crazy.

"She was having a dream. She doesn't know what she's saying." Uncle Toddy pushed my brother away. "She'll be fine in the morning. Go to bed, Rich."

Honey was crying. I was crying too.

Uncle Toddy waited until Richie was gone. Then he spoke, his voice rigid with anger.

"Listen to me, Carolyn. I don't know what's gotten into you lately, but I'm not putting up with this kind of abuse. I don't know where you're getting this vampire stuff, but it's sick, it's stupid, it makes you look crazy. Haven't we got enough problems in this house? Richie's strung out on drugs—you think I don't know that? I'm trying to help him. He's got real problems, unlike yours. You're making up all this shit in your mind. Why? For fun? Or just to be difficult? You worry all the time. You never eat. I make all your favorite foods and you don't even touch them—"

"I'm sorry," Honey whimpered. "I was having a bad dream. A monster was chasing me and I was so scared and I couldn't get away, but then I woke up."

"That's all right, Honey." He turned gentle again. "It

could happen to anyone. It's not your fault. Do you want me to stay here until you fall asleep?"

"No, thank you. I'm fine."

Sometimes I could strangle her baby voice.

Then I noticed something I never had before. How could I have been so blind? There was no lock on our bedroom door. Anyone could walk in, anytime.

"I want to put a lock on the door," I said.

"I wouldn't if I were you," he said. "It wouldn't be safe, in case of a fire."

"We haven't had too many fires lately."

"It only takes one," my uncle replied.

"I could jump out the window and climb down the tree."

"Yeah, or maybe you could fly." Uncle Toddy rubbed his face. "I'm not going to stand here and argue with you, Carolyn. It's late. We'll talk about it in the morning. Good night, Honey."

"Good night," she said.

He went out and closed the door behind him.

I turned on the light and said, "We've got to talk."

"I'm not talking to you. You get us in trouble."

"You're the one who was screaming and sobbing!"

"Yes, because you scare me all the time! I can't concentrate in school! Things are falling apart! If my grades don't improve, I can't be a cheerleader! Ms. Johnson called me into her office!"

Ms. Johnson is the school counselor. I visited her office recently too. I didn't tell Honey; she would have worried. There are so many things she can't face.

Ms. Johnson told me that my teachers are concerned. The quality of my work is deteriorating. If I don't improve my grades, I'll have trouble getting into college. Also, I'll get kicked out of the play. You have to maintain a decent grade-point average in order to participate in extracurricular activities.

This had never been a problem for me before. I've always gotten A's. Ms. Johnson was talking D's and incompletes. I was shocked to find myself in her office. I felt as if we were discussing someone else's life.

"Is anything wrong, Carolyn?" she'd asked. "Are you having problems at home?"

"Everything's fine," I told her. "I'm just real busy. With school and the play and everything."

"Don't tell Mama about my grades!" Honey plucked at her tangled hair. "There's no sense getting her all upset. I'll quit my job so I can study on Saturdays." She's been working at a flower shop, for spending money.

"Relax," I said. "Will you calm down? Just try a little harder."

"I'm trying as hard as I can!"

"So quit being a cheerleader. Who cares?"

"I do! Why do you make fun of everything I like? I don't make fun of you, or the play. Anyway, I don't want to be like you. You're never happy. You're crazy."

"You ought to know."

"I'm going to sleep. Don't talk to me. Just leave me alone."

I heard muffled conversation downstairs. I turned off the light, opened my door, and crept to the top of the stairs where I could hear.

"No, I don't think so," my uncle was saying.

Papa said something; I couldn't make out the words.

"No, she's fine. But Carolyn's been under a strain."

Why am I always the bad guy, the villain? Sweet little Honey can do no wrong. That dimpled darling. That bloodless birdbrain. That blubbering, simpering, whimpering shit. Sometimes I wish Honey were dead. Sometimes I could kill her.

Mama said something, but her voice was too soft.

"It's this college thing," Uncle Toddy explained. "She's worried about her grades. You know what a hard worker she is. And she's got all those after-school activities."

Mama murmured something. My father exploded. "What good do they do? They're a bunch of quacks! And they cost an arm and a leg."

"I don't think she needs a psychiatrist," Uncle Toddy said. "Not yet. But we need to keep an eye on the situation. Make sure she eats, gets plenty of rest, and has some fun. All she does is study. I was thinking of taking her to the coast some weekend. Just the two of us. She used to love that."

I almost howled with laughter.

"You know how kids are," Uncle Toddy was saying. "They all go through it. I was a handful myself. Well, Bill, you remember. The folks called me the hellion. Don't worry about Carolyn. She'll be fine. I just thought you'd like to know what all the commotion was about."

I slid back into our bedroom and closed the door. Then I pushed a chair in front of it, with the wastebasket on top. If I fell asleep reading and the door was opened, the wastebasket would wake me when it hit the floor.

But he didn't come back. He went into his room. After a while I sensed that everyone was sleeping. I turned off the light and stepped into the hall, my knife cool and hard in my hands.

I glided through the moonlit rooms downstairs. The grandfather clock was ticking, ticking. Honey's piano grinned, showing its teeth.

I floated through the dining room and into the kitchen, where a locked door leads down to the cellar and my uncle's workshop. The lock was placed high, out of reach of little hands, to keep us from falling down the stairs when we were small.

My knife undid the screws that held the lock in place. Removing it left tiny holes in the wood, but Mama wouldn't notice. There is so much she doesn't notice.

Then I slipped upstairs and into our room. I used

my knife to screw the lock into the doorframe. When I slid the metal pin in place, my heart almost burst, it was so full of relief. We were finally safe. We could rest in peace.

I wasn't worried about fire. If a fire broke out, we could open the window and climb down the tree. It's a long way to the ground below. I tried climbing down once, when Uncle Toddy came after me. He grabbed me and wrapped me in his wings.

I got into bed and pulled up the covers. Then I turned off the light and fell asleep; not curled up like a fist, but as relaxed as a baby resting in her mama's arms. Nothing could harm us now. We were free.

When I came home from school the next day, the lock was gone.

Rehearsal ran late. I couldn't stay in character. I kept forgetting who I was supposed to be. I felt as if I were sitting in the back of the dark auditorium, watching a blond girl pretending to be Carolyn pretending to be someone else.

At one point, Mrs. Bennett said, "Earth to Carolyn. Do you read me?" and the cast members laughed. It was embarrassing.

I've thought about quitting the play, but it's too late; our first performance is a month away. Acting used to be a vacation, an escape.

Now I'm acting all the time.

When I got home, Uncle Toddy said, "You got some mail," and handed me a letter from Maggie. My heart leaped at the sight of her familiar scribble.

The envelope was unsealed.

"I'm sorry," Uncle Toddy said. "I thought it was for me. Don't worry. I didn't read it. How was school?"

"Fine." I took the letter upstairs and sat on my bed and began to read.

Dear Carrie,

I decided to write you a letter because I can't seem to get you on the phone. I called the other night, but you were sleeping.

I talked to Uncle Toddy. He said you've been feeling kind of burned out, worrying about school and everything.

You get a 4.0! What more do you want? And you've got tons of extra activities. Colleges will be knocking down your door! When the time comes, I'll help you figure out all those stupid applications. Ms. Johnson can help you too. She was great; told me about the scholarships, loans, grants, etc.

You worry too much, kid! Take it easy.

You are listening to the Voice of Experience, broadcasting live on station KBFD, from Boston, Massachusetts.

I wish you could come back east sometime. You'd love it here, Carrie. It's so beautiful in the fall. The leaves on the trees turn incredible colors. I mean orange. A few weeks ago some friends and I drove up into Vermont. There are all these little villages, too perfect to be real: rolling green lawns, old farmhouses, tiny white churches, and corner stores stuffed with everything you could possibly need, from bunion pads to sleigh bells. I even found some of those big red cinnamon balls like Grammy used to have in the pantry, remember? She kept them up high, in that big brown crock, where we (supposedly) couldn't reach them.

Which reminds me: I confess. I'm the one who kept eating the Tang. I dug it out of the jar with a spoon. You little guys always took the rap. I owe you.

This is my last year of school, theoretically. But I've decided (don't tell Papa yet) that I don't want to be an English teacher. I'm going to go for my M.A., so I can be (drum roll, please) a counselor; specifically, an M.F.C.C., which means Marriage, Family, and Children's Counselor. There's only about five million of them already. But that's okay, because the world needs us.

I think I would be a good counselor. I like people (most people) and am pretty good at figuring out what makes them tick. To me, that's the most fascinating thing there is—people and their stories.

Papa will think it's hogwash. He was never too crazy (yuk yuk) about all those shrinks who treated Mama, and frankly, I'm not sure they helped. There are good therapists and bad ones. Some people get into the profession because they're so messed up themselves that they need the illusion (delusion) of being in control: an expert.

I don't think that's my problem. I've gotten some counseling, mostly in groups run through the college, and it's really been helpful. I wish you'd consider it, if you're feeling down in the dumps. At first it's scary because you're afraid that if you say how you feel, or what you think, people will think you're nuts. But they don't. Anyway, it's been good for me. There was so much I had to figure out, about our family.

I always told people (and myself) that my childhood was perfect. But it wasn't. I don't know if you've noticed this, but our family is a little, uh, how should I put this, strange. Depressing. That's the word. Depressed. It's like there's an invisible cloud over our house. The family fog. You can't see it, but it sure gets in your face.

When I was a kid I couldn't understand why our house felt so different than my friends' houses. Not that their families didn't have problems too. My psych professor says that most American families are dysfunctional, to one degree or another.

Our family is dysfunctional to the nth degree. The tenth power. I know you'll think I'm disloyal for saying that. But the longer I'm away from home, the clearer it becomes to me.

It's not like I remember bad things happening, like murder or mayhem or screaming. It's more what didn't happen. Something was missing. Fun. It was always so tense there, know what I mean? We never knew when Mama might get worse, or why, and Papa was always so worried.

But nobody talked about it! That was the weirdest thing of all! The situation was never discussed. No matter what was happening, we pretended things were great. I guess they thought we were too little to notice. An ambulance comes and takes Mama away, and what does Papa say? "Finish your dinner."!!!

For all us kids knew, it was all our fault. Maybe we'd driven her insane, that's what I thought. Mama wasn't cut out to have children. Parakeets, maybe; gold-fish, sure; but not kids. One minute she's there, and she's crying a lot, and suddenly she's gone, and Papa and Uncle Toddy don't want to talk about her. If you asked where she was, they said: "Mama's fine," but the look on their faces said she'd died. Then she comes back from the hospital, or Mars, or wherever the hell she was, and it's like nothing ever happened. We pretended she was never gone. Suddenly everything's supposed to be peachy—except we're tiptoeing around the house like it's a minefield.

Maybe this sounds crazy to you. I don't mean to sound so negative. I know Mama and Papa love us, but they're not too good at showing it. They've got too many problems of their own. When you're little, you think all adults are like God, but some of them are just big children. (Papa would flip if he read this. He hates all this "psychology shit." His words, not mine.)

When I was a kid I thought all families were like ours. Then I'd go to some of my friends' houses, and the families would be laughing and joking and hugging. I'd think: If I was a good kid, my parents would love me. So I tried and tried to be so good, but nothing changed.

I couldn't wait to leave. I know that sounds cold. I know everybody was hurt when I chose a college so far away. But I had to do it, Carrie. Sometimes you need to leave a place to understand where you've been.

Don't get me wrong: I love our family. But we're not the healthiest bunch of bananas in the world.

I can hear what you're thinking. You think I've changed. You're right, Carrie. And I'm glad.

I'm sorry I couldn't come back last summer. I know you wanted to see me, and I wanted to see you too. But I had to work. (The tips are good. Number-one tip: Don't be a waitress.) And frankly, I didn't want to come home. This is my home now. I like it here. I have lots of great friends, and I'm seeing this guy. Nothing serious yet, but he's wonderful, Carrie. His name is Michael Brooks. We have so much fun. I wish you could meet him. Maybe you can visit this summer. I could take some time off and we could talk and talk, and go to the Cape, and drive up into New Hampshire and swim in the lakes there. You'd love it.

I'm sorry I won't be home for Christmas. I can't afford the plane fare and neither can Papa. I gather from what Uncle Toddy said that things aren't going too hot for Papa financially. Everything is so expensive now! I can't believe how much stuff costs.

Please write and let me know how you are. I'm sorry I missed you the other night. I didn't think you'd be in bed so early. The time difference makes things confusing. I'll try again sometime soon.

Don't let this letter bum you out. I'm trying to be close to you, Carrie: to say what's in my heart and

*mind, so that I'm not a familiar stranger. I want you to
really know me, and I want to know you too. Please
give my love to all the family, and save a big bunch for
yourself.*

> *Your beautiful and extremely wise big sister,*
> *Maggie*

I folded up the letter and set it on my pillow. I felt
so odd. My breath came quickly. Maggie was not coming home for Christmas. Maggie was not coming home
again. This was not her home. She had turned her back
and walked away, as if our family was an accident, a
bloody fatality, a tragic wreck. How could she desert
me? I wasn't dead! I was alive, and I needed her so
badly.

I picked up the letter and read it again, then held it
to my face. Maggie had touched this letter with her
hands. Maggie still loved me; it said so on the paper.
Maggie would always be my sister.

I let Honey read the letter. She said I was overreacting. She said: "That's what happens when people go
away to college. They think they know everything."

She and Maggie have never been close. They don't
have much in common. Maggie always regarded cheerleading as if it were a joke. "It has nothing to do with
skill or talent," she said. "It's just a popularity contest."
Honey says Maggie feels that way because she wasn't

pretty or popular. Which is true. She was incredibly wonderful and funny and smart, none of which counts for much at our high school.

At dinnertime, Richie didn't come to the table. He said he didn't feel like eating.

Papa started steaming. But Uncle Toddy said, "It's all right, Bill. Rich and I have an understanding."

Mama said to me, "I hear you got a letter from Maggie."

"Nice of her to take the time to write," Papa said. He was being sarcastic. I wish people would say what they mean. Sometimes I feel like I'm going to start screaming. But if I said: "Can we all please be honest for once?" they'd say: "What on earth are you talking about, Carolyn? The problem is yours, not ours. If there were a problem, which of course there's not."

I said, "She can't afford to come home for Christmas."

"Oh, that's too bad." Mama looked disappointed.

"Let me serve you, Doris." Uncle Toddy filled her plate.

"I'm really not that hungry." Mama picked up her fork and ate.

"I slave all day over a hot stove, and this is the thanks I get!" Uncle Toddy mimed exasperation. "How about you, Honey?"

"I'm starving," she said. He heaped her plate with potatoes, meat, and salad. "Mmm, it looks delicious."

She eats like a pig. Sometimes I can't bear to have her near me.

"She didn't have to go to college back east," Papa said around a mouthful of steak. "She could've gone out here. I can't afford to fly her all over the country. That tuition is killing me."

"What about her scholarships and grants? Those help." But Papa didn't hear me. Had I said the words aloud, or only thought them?

"Kids have to get away," said Uncle Toddy. "You remember, Bill. You were young once."

"About a million years ago," Papa said. Honey giggled. Laughing at his jokes improves his mood.

I ate in silence, watching my uncle. I knew that he had read Maggie's letter. Would he tell my parents all the things she had written?

I said, "Why didn't you tell me that Maggie called me?"

"I'm sorry," he said. "I forgot."

"You should've woken me up. I wanted to talk to her."

"You need your sleep. More meat, Bill? I'll get it." Uncle Toddy winked at me and went into the kitchen.

We are down in the cellar, Uncle Toddy and I. The cellar is as dark and as private as sleep.

He is honing his claws on a spinning silver wheel. Sparks fly off and glitter in his hair.

I could call out to my family, but no one would hear me. Uncle Toddy says they went away on vacation.

Why did they forget to take me with them?

I promise I won't get carsick anymore, or say I have to stop and pee. I promise I won't fight with the other kids!

"Don't cry," he says. "They'll be back someday. Don't you want to stay with me?"

I want to say no, but my tongue fills my throat. His voice has little razor teeth. I used to love to listen to him talk, but now my ears are bleeding.

"As soon as I'm done we can have some fun. I've built you this boat," Uncle Toddy tells me.

I'm sitting in the boat. It's tight like a kayak, with a fitted top, in case it rains. I don't like the top down; too close, I can't breathe. He folds it back. He's good with his hands. He makes gifts for the family; a bookshelf for Mama, a wine rack for Papa, a rocking horse for Honey and me. The wood's not smooth. There's a splinter in my hand. Uncle Toddy plucks it out with his teeth.

I am so confused. Is this day or night? There are no windows in the cellar. No natural light. Uncle Toddy's face glows. His skin is so white. His black cape covers his folded wings. The cape is lined with scarlet silk that feels like skin. My skin. I'm shrinking. I'm just a baby, just a little girl, drowning in my hair; it floods the boat, it leaks over the side, spills along the floor, a yellow tide rising toward the spinning wheel.

Stop! It's caught! My scalp is ripping off!

Uncle Toddy saves me. He untangles my hair. His polished claws gently rake my face.

"Almost done," he says, "then we'll have some fun. Don't my hands look pretty?"

"Oh, yes," I say, but I mean, oh no. His fingernails curve like question marks. Why am I so small? I'm not a baby. I want to leave the cellar. I want to escape. But the stairs to the kitchen have disappeared.

"All finished," Uncle Toddy says. "Let's go for a ride in your new boat." He climbs in and sits behind me.

"I can't," I say. "I don't know how to swim."

That doesn't matter. Uncle Toddy will save me. Even if he has to throw me in.

"I want to take you out on the lake," he says.

There's no water in the cellar, so we must be pretending. I know about make-believe. My parents say I have a vivid imagination. They make it sound like a disease. It can be, when it's hard to tell what's real, especially when you're little and nobody believes you.

I wanted to go with them, but they left me here. Why don't they love me? I promise I'll be good!

"There's no water," I say. As usual, I'm wrong. The floor dissolves into a stream. Uncle Toddy slips an oar into the water and guides the canoe through a hole in the wall. We enter a tunnel. It is narrow and damp.

"Where are we going? Are we in the house?" It's so dark. We must be inside the walls, moving through the water pipes.

"Close your eyes," Uncle Toddy says. "I want to surprise you."

"I have to pee." He doesn't hear me, although he's sitting so close his chest is pressed against my back. It's become hard to tell if I am talking or just thinking

"Carolyn, are you afraid of me?"

"No," I say. That was true, long ago. Things were different then, and so was he.

Now I see his teeth. He's not the person I knew. Which one is the real Uncle Toddy?

"The world is a strange place," he murmurs in my ear, as if he were reading my mind. "A strange place full of strangers. Do you understand?"

"Yes," I say. I always say yes. Especially when I don't know what he means.

"Friends are fine, but they come and go. Family is blood," he says. "Blood is forever. That's why you're so special to me."

"Like Grammy," I say. He's afraid of Grammy. He

cringes when I mention her name. Suddenly I want her so desperately that, wherever she is, she must feel my longing. "I want Grammy!" I cry.

"Don't be a baby. Aren't you having fun? Aren't you having a good time?"

"Yes," I say, so he won't be angry. "But I can't see."

"Of course you can't. Open your eyes." His voice becomes gentle. "Carolyn, have you ever seen anything so pretty?"

The picture's inside out. It's a negative, silver defining the shapes of shadows. The lake we are riding is high in the sky. The moon is a ball shining up through the water. Trees by the shore wave their roots in the air. Or is that women with tangled hair? The sky is alive with fish. No, I've got it all turned around. The world isn't upside down; it's me. I see. It's the reflections on the water.

"I'm all mixed up," I say, turning to Uncle Toddy. In his place is a giant red insect.

"No!" I'm screaming. "No, don't bite me!"

"For God's sake, Carolyn, I was only kidding!" Uncle Toddy removes his insect mask. "See?"

I can't stop crying. I call for Grammy. I'm saying the prayer she taught me: "Our Father, who art in heaven—"

"Quit that," Uncle Toddy says. "You sound like an old lady."

"I want to go home!"

"You *are* home," he says. "Lower your voice. Do you want to get in trouble? Grammy would be mad. You're not supposed to be out at night, especially in your nightgown. You've got nothing on your feet. Where are your slippers?"

He's right, of course, Grammy would be disappointed. She wouldn't say so, but her eyes would tell me. I can't afford to lose her; she's the only one who loves me. I don't want him to see me cry, but I can't help it.

"Poor baby." Uncle Toddy puts his strong arms around me, careful not to scratch me with his claws. "I didn't mean to scare you. It was just a joke. See, this mask looks like a bug." He starts to put it on again.

"Don't hurt me!"

"I wouldn't hurt you. Have I ever hurt you? I would never hurt you," Uncle Toddy says. "The thing is— stop crying and listen to me, Carolyn—the thing is, you're a vampire now too, and you might as well get used to it."

"I'm not!" I want to jump into the lake, but I would never make it back to shore.

"Yes, you are, Carolyn. You're a vampire too. You know how it works; you've seen the movies. But it's not so bad. In fact, you'll love it. You'll never get old; you'll stay young like me. And it's not like we're evil. We don't kill anybody. The thing is, people have more blood than they need. That's why they leave some at blood banks. Really. All we want is a taste. We don't hurt anybody."

"What about the others? Don't hurt my mother!"

"Do you think I'm a monster? I would never hurt your mama. And you mustn't hurt her either," Uncle Toddy says sincerely. "You're so negative and crabby. That worries her, Carolyn. She's got a lot on her mind. How do you think she'd feel if she found out you were a vampire? What would Gram think?"

"They'd hate it!" I cry.

"They might even make you go away. They wouldn't understand. People have the wrong idea about vampires. This is our secret. You and I know the truth."

His eyes pierce mine. His wings are rising. His mouth falls open like a rotting wound.

"I don't want to die!"

I wake up, shrieking, to the circle of faces: Richie, Mama, Papa, Uncle Toddy; even Grammy and Grampa are crowded around my bed.

"She's coming out of it now," Papa says.

Mama says: "Carolyn, you had us so worried."

Grammy doesn't say a thing. Her face is ancient with sadness.

"I was having a dream—" But it's all jumbled up. I can't explain where I've been or what I've seen.

Uncle Toddy says, "Sweetie, you've been under a strain. That's all over now. You're safe. We're here."

"Where's Honey?"

"Asleep," Papa says. "Don't wake her. She's so worried about you. We all are, Carolyn. You're not yourself."

"Where's Margaret?" I ask. "I need to talk to Maggie!"

Their eyebrows shoot skyward like startled birds.

"She's three thousand miles away," Papa says. "In Boston. Don't you remember?"

"Of course I remember! Get her on the phone! I need to talk to Maggie!"

Richie looks scared. He doesn't say a word.

I say, "I dreamed I was dying. I couldn't find you. You all went away on vacation."

"I'm sorry," Mama says. "It's all my fault. It's in the genes. That's why you're acting so strange."

"I'm not crazy!"

"You're not to blame. Don't worry anymore. It's all arranged."

"What's arranged?" I sit up in bed. "What're you talking about?"

"The hospital." Papa avoids looking into my eyes.

"Don't worry." Uncle Toddy strokes my hair. "The ambulance is on its way."

I pull away from his hands. "What's the matter with you people? Has everybody gone crazy?"

"Don't be scared," Grampa says. "You'll be home for Christmas. We'll come and see you every day."

"There's nothing wrong with me! I'm not going anywhere! You're the ones who are crazy!"

"Pills," Uncle Toddy says. "She needs some tranquilizers."

"Not too many," Richie says. "They're strong."

Fear crashes through me. I'm running through my veins, running down halls lined with locked doors, shrieking: "No, you've got to listen! This house is poisoned! He's killing us! We're all infected!"

"What are you talking about?" Papa's face is angry.

"Uncle Toddy is a vampire! He's drinking our blood!"

My grandmother collapses on the floor, dead.

"Now look what you've done! You've killed her!" Papa says.

Mama covers her face with her hands and turns away.

I'm kicking and screaming. Uncle Toddy holds me down.

"For God's sake!" he shouts. "Where's the ambulance?

He's shaking me and shaking me. My eyes snap open. Richie's frightened face is close, his hands are on my shoulders.

"Wake up!" he says. "Wake up! You're dreaming!"

But how can I be sure?

Honey and I were learning to drive. She was at the steering wheel and I was in the backseat, keeping my mouth shut. She's not the world's best driver. She jerks the steering wheel this way, that way, then slams on the brakes at the stop sign: *Errrrrrr!*

Mr. Robinson, who also teaches math, told her she was doing fine. He likes Honey. She twinkles and dimples and laughs at his jokes, and doesn't say a word when he pats her knee.

Hey, it's her knee, not mine.

"Turn left at the corner," Mr. Robinson said.

Honey tapped the brake. We st-st-st-stopped at the signal light.

"You don't have to brake so soon," he said.

"I'm sorry," Honey said. "I'm so excited."

She could hardly sit still. She was practically twitching. *I'm a big girl now! I'm learning to drive! I could see her reflection in the rearview mirror, her face wildly happy, her eyes shining. She steered that car as if it were her life and she was finally in control.

Honey doesn't know that she's circling a track that will take her back to where she started.

"Yield," Robinson said. "The sign said 'yield.'"

Honey yielded and merged and zipped down the road, waving to friends ("Keep your hands on the wheel!"), humming like a little blond engine.

I cringed in the backseat. Cars and trucks were all around us. A foot or two closer and we'd be squashed. Let Honey drive. I don't want to take my turn. I know I should learn; it would free me.

If I knew how to drive, I could leave this town. A memory stirs in its sleep. We ran away. We were small. It was dark. We were wearing pajamas and slippers. Maggie buttoned up our coats and put scarves on our heads. It was cold. It was winter.

Someone was shouting in the living room. Papa? Arguing with Mama? With Uncle Toddy?

"Come on," Maggie said. We slipped out the front door. Nobody noticed; they were too busy yelling.

We hurried down the sidewalk, under huge, heavy trees, their branches thrashing in the wind. It felt so odd to be out at night—like Halloween, without the candy.

"Hold hands," Maggie said. We all held hands.

Richie started crying. "The police will get us."

"Don't be a baby," Maggie said. "Hurry up."

She was taking us to Grammy's house. Grammy would know what to do. She would make them stop yelling.

Then we came to the end of the block, where the avenue broadens, at the intersection. I looked up at Maggie's face, so strong and brave, shining in the street-light. Then her mouth twisted.

"We can't cross the street," she announced flatly. "Not till we're older. They said so."

We didn't argue, of course, because Maggie was the boss. There was no place to go, so we went back. We had to ring the doorbell. They were surprised to see us. Mama and Papa and Uncle Toddy got mad at us; especially at Maggie, because she was the oldest and should've known better.

That memory appeared like a photograph as Honey drove through that same intersection.

"You're doing fine," Robinson said. He sneaks looks at her legs when he thinks she won't notice. It makes her nervous, so she pretends to be unconscious, one of her specialties. She's wearing a miniskirt. Her legs are long and curvy. She'd deny it, but she likes people to notice her body.

It was my turn to drive. "You're doing great," Robinson told me.

"I like to drive." That would please Honey. I've been trying not to rock her boat. "It's weird, when you think how close the other cars are."

"What do you mean?"

"I mean, we could get killed any second."

"Not that we will," Honey added.

"Don't think about that," Robinson said. "Just watch the road."

As we walked home, Honey was practically skipping.

"That was fun," she said. "I can't wait to drive."

"Drive what?"

"Mama's car, I guess."

"Uncle Toddy's always got it, since his truck broke down. Why doesn't he get it fixed?"

"He doesn't have any money."

"Why not? He's got a job."

"Do you think Papa will pay for our insurance?"

"I doubt it. In case you haven't noticed, his business is going down the drain."

"No, it's not," Honey said. "The insurance won't cost much. You get a discount if your grades are good."

"They're not. Remember?"

"They will be." Honey kicked brown leaves along the sidewalk.

I dropped the subject. I didn't want to spoil her mood. Things are going pretty smoothly. Tonight she's going to the homecoming dance with our school's star quarterback, Curtis Bradley. Or is it Bradley Curtis? I can never remember.

Uncle Toddy had a snack of cheese and crackers waiting for Honey. She'll have dinner in a restaurant before the dance.

"I'm not hungry, Uncle Toddy."

He pouted. She ate.

She's happy tonight. She's in love with Curtis Bradley. Our team won the homecoming game. Wahoo. She's sailing up into the sky like a pink balloon, her hope carrying her high above the ground. It scares me.

She stood before the mirror, piling up her hair, then letting it splash, thick and golden, down her back. She wants to look perfect for Curtis Bradley. Bradley Curtis. Whatever.

He's not your average jock. He's intelligent and kind. He's nice to people who aren't even popular. Even Janis Simms, the official school fat girl. There must always be a fat girl for everyone to torture.

Someday Janis Simms will return for our class re-union, a beautiful woman, in a size six dress, carrying an Oscar. Or a machine gun, perhaps.

I can't stay on track. I was talking about Bradley. Or Curtis. Maybe there're two of him, like us. We could double-date. Honey wouldn't like that. She prefers to keep her friends and my friends separate.

Trying to be objective, I watched Honey dress, thinking: Who is that girl? What would a stranger see?

She could be a model. A magazine cover girl. The all-American fashion doll: blue eyes, red lips, blond hair. She hates her nose; she thinks it spoils her looks. She covered it with her hand and stared into the mirror.

I said, "You could walk around like that all night." She stuck out her tongue at me.

She looks shorter than I do, by an inch or two.

Honey projects petiteness. Her gown is made of dark blue velvet. It's a simple dress, sweeping to the floor, baring her shoulders and back. And front.

I said: "You'll fall out of that dress." I would never wear a strapless, my breasts served up. Please help yourself.

"All the girls are wearing them. Even Nancy," Honey said. She's double-dating with Nancy and Bobby Sloane.

Honey's not sorry that I won't be attending. She's glad that I'm staying home. She says I'm too critical.

"You look beautiful," I said when she was finally ready.

She made an awful face in the mirror. Honey craves compliments but fears they're a trick. If she said, "Gee, thanks," you might scream, "Just kidding!"

She has no idea why people think she's pretty.

Curtis Bradley arrived, shockingly handsome in his tux. If he and Honey get married someday, they will have the world's most gorgeous children.

He had an orchid for Honey. She wore it in her hair; there wasn't room on the front of her dress. Bradley talked to Papa. Uncle Toddy took pictures. Richie went out, letting the front door bang. Before he left, he kissed my cheek.

There's something important that I'm trying to re-member. I can't hold my mind in place. It keeps slip-

ping away. What was I saying? What is it that I mustn't
forget? I remember that I must remember something,
but it scuttles out of sight when I turn my head, darting
into darkness, like mice. There are so many places to
hide in this house, so many holes and crevices. I've told
Papa about the mice. We could get a cat. But Mama
says cats are dirty. Uncle Toddy put out poison.

I'm supposed to be working on a paper for English.
It's due very soon. Or was it due last week? Once things
start unraveling, it's hard to stop them, like that sweater
I had; I pulled one loose loop and it all came undone,
a pile of yarn. So it's important to fix things when they
first go wrong. Before they have a chance to completely
break down.

That is what I'm trying to remember. That is what I
must not forget. I have got to pay attention. I keep
writing things down here. So I won't let myself forget
to remember. And if I die, someone will know what
happened.

"Oh, please!" Honey would say. "Must we be so
dramatic?" She'd think it was a joke. Or tear this up.
She'd say: "Don't put your craziness in writing. You
might as well hold up a sign that says: *I'm nuts!*"

Honey doesn't know about this journal.

I can picture her at the homecoming dance. Oh, she
is having such a fabulous time, surrounded by her
friends. They're talking and laughing, and Bradley has
his arm around her waist; not tight. Just right. The

band is playing her favorite songs, as if the musicians were reading her mind.

The cafeteria is so dark you can't see where you are; it's an elegant ballroom, in a castle in France. And wouldn't you know it! Curtis and Honey are chosen as the king and queen of the homecoming dance!

They're up on the stage wearing golden crowns, and Honey is holding an armful of roses. It's so perfect, you know, because they're the perfect couple; she's the prettiest cheerleader, and he's the handsomest quarterback, and the football team has won every game!

The crowd applauds and roars its approval. Honey stands in the warmth of the spotlight, smiling and waving, smiling and waving.

I liked Thanksgiving when Maggie was around. When we were little we drew turkeys and pilgrims. She'd let me use her big box of crayons. Their points were always crisp, like her.

She called to wish us a happy Thanksgiving.

I took the call on the phone in the kitchen. I could hear people laughing and talking in the background.

"Carrie, how are you?"

"Fine. How are you?"

"Great! Will you get that thing away from me? They're torturing me with a frozen turkey! You guys know I'm a vegetarian! Now it's flying around the room." She was talking to her friends and roommates. When had Maggie become a vegetarian?

Uncle Toddy took the phone. "How's it going, kiddo? Had any snow yet?" After him, Mama took the call on the phone in her bedroom.

We had company coming in the afternoon, Papa's sister Marion and her family. They live a few hours away. We hardly ever see them. Papa and Aunt Marion don't like each other, so they get together only on special occasions. Which seems odd, since they wouldn't take each other out for lunch.

There was a lot to do before the guests arrived. Papa built a big fire in the living room. Then he started vacuuming. Richie raked leaves in the front yard. It was cold, but he wouldn't wear a jacket.

He pushed the leaves into a pile and tried to burn them. Papa rapped on the window and shook his head. "No!" he kept shouting. "They won't burn! They're too wet!" Richie pretended not to hear him. He doused the leaves with lighter fluid and got them going, but they smoldered. Thick gray smoke rolled toward the house.

"See? What did I tell you!" Papa shouted, vindicated.

Mama was in the kitchen, whipping cream to top the pumpkin pies she'd bought at the supermarket. She'd washed her hair. It was curly and wet. She used to be beautiful. I've seen her pictures. She looked a lot like Honey.

Now there's a jagged line between her eyebrows that looks like a tiny lightning bolt. Her hair has gone dark and ordinary. But she's not fat like a lot of parents. She could look really good if she tried.

"You look nice, Mama. I like that dress." It was a soft knit, the color of raspberry sherbet.

"Thank you, sweetie. Aren't you going to get dressed?"

"I will." I was wearing the gray sweats I'd slept in. "I want to get some work done first."

I washed celery and stuffed it with cream cheese. I filled crystal bowls with olives and nuts. Honey helped Uncle Toddy get the turkey ready for the oven, plunging handfuls of stuffing into its hollow belly. She loves it when company comes to the house, because we all make a special effort to act normal.

Mama was in a jolly mood. She hummed while she peeled the squash. Uncle Toddy went upstairs to get dressed. It was a perfect opportunity for me and Mama to talk. We seldom do. Uncle Toddy is always listening. He could be a spy for the FBI. He's probably outside the kitchen right now, waiting to hear what I'm going to tell her.

I could say: "Mama, why don't we ever talk?"

"What do you mean?" she'd reply.

"We never talk."

"Talk about what?" She'd still be smiling, hoping I was being silly.

"Stuff that matters," I'd say.

"Stuff like what?" The smile would be fading; she'd get really busy.

"Mama, I have good news and bad news."

"Don't tell me the bad news," she'd whisper.

"The bad news is, Uncle Toddy's a vampire. The good news is, I may be imagining it. In which case, I'm completely nuts."

Mama could feel me getting ready to speak. She moved around the kitchen quickly.

Then she looked directly at me.

"Nothing's wrong, is there, Carolyn?"

"No. I was just thinking."

"What do you suppose your brother's doing? It smells like he's burning down the neighborhood."

"I hope so."

She smiled at me and fled from the kitchen. I pictured Richie loping from house to house, christening each one with lighter fluid; in the name of the Father, the Son, the Holy Ghost.

Which reminds me: I'm supposed to write and deliver a Thanksgiving grace. I've done that since I was a little girl.

Maybe I would ask Honey to do it. She was bustling around, being useful. Uncle Toddy, is there anything I can do? Could I pour you a glass of blood?

Grammy says forgiveness is the soul of a true Christian. But how can I forgive the unforgivable?

Sensing tension in our happy home (what a mind she has, she's so perceptive!), Honey skipped to the piano and played "Jesu Joy of Man's Desiring." She played exquisitely. Everyone stopped bickering and listened.

"That was wonderful, Honey," Papa said when she was finished. "Rich, help me get the extra chairs." Uplifted by the music, he added, "please." Honey beamed with relief.

Richie drove over to pick up Gram and Grampa. In the old days, Gram would've been here early, cooking up a storm.

Sometimes I feel angry at her. I want to grab her and shout: "Don't get old! Don't die!" We used to have such good times together. We picked armloads of daisies in the field behind her house. That field is full of apartments now. Gram played dolls with me for hours. We sang songs about Jesus, and she told me funny stories about Mama's mischief when she was a little girl. I'd lie on the couch beside Grammy and giggle.

That's all over now. Richie guided Grammy and Gramps into the house. They came in slowly and sat by the fire.

"Carolyn, you look splendid!" Grammy said. "Honey, I love that dress. Richie, dear, would you hand me my purse? Thank you, dear. I need some tissue. Wouldn't it be wonderful if Margaret could be with us?"

"She called this morning," Mama said, and related the conversation.

Our relatives arrived. Papa and Aunt Marion gave each other smacking kisses. Papa's voice gets loud when he greets his sister and her husband, Uncle Wayne, and their teenage sons, Mark and Damon.

We all swam around like fish in a tank. There was lots of talking and snacking and noise. A football game blared on the TV. I circulated with appetizers and brought Gram and Gramps cups of decaffeinated coffee, which is also the only kind that Mama drinks. She claims caffeine ruins her sleep.

Papa, Uncle Wayne, and Uncle Toddy watched the football game. Once in a while they jumped up, shouting: "Yes!" Richie smoked cigarettes on the porch with

Damon. Mark, who's thirteen, rode Richie's old skate-board up and down the driveway.

I hung out with Richie and Damon for a while. When you talk to Damon, he won't look you in the eye. He glances at his feet or off to the side. Richie does that too. He didn't used to.

There was a nip in the air, so I went back inside. Mama and Aunt Marion were at the dining room table, talking about how expensive everything is these days, and how crummy things are made; they fall apart as soon as you make the last payment.

"Good thing for you!" Uncle Wayne boomed in his wife's ear. "If it weren't for that, I'd be out of business!" Uncle Wayne owns a car dealership.

"You might be out of business anyway, if the econ-omy doesn't pick up," Papa said.

"You're telling me." Uncle Wayne nodded grimly.

"How's business, Bill?" Aunt Marion asked abruptly.

"Just fine," Papa said. "I can't complain."

Papa thinks Aunt Marion is too critical, that she never has a good word to say. The same could be said for him. He's always on Richie. Would I like my father if I didn't love him? He was drinking beer and getting louder. His belly strained the waistband of his pants. When people disagree with him or interrupt his mono-logues on the Trouble with Foreigners, or the Econ-omy's a Disgrace, he turns up the volume and drowns them out.

"He's a dog!" he shouted at Uncle Wayne, referring to the coach of a football team. "They're paying him a million and a half to lose! I wish I had a deal like that!"

"Yeah, you're losing for nothing," said Aunt Marion. Papa laughed hard at her joke.

You can tell when Aunt Marion's going to say something sharp because her mouth puckers up, as if she's blowing a dart.

She said, "Richie seems a little withdrawn."

The barb was so pointed Mama barely felt it. Then the poison entered her bloodstream. Aunt Marion was saying that Richie is rude.

(*"He's not rude!"* I wanted to scream. *"He just can't stand you!"*)

Mama glanced toward the porch. Richie slumped on the railing. His long blond hair needed washing.

"He's shy," Mama explained.

"How's he doing in school?"

"Oh, fine," Mama said. "He's going to graduate in June. Can you believe it? The time goes so quickly."

"What's he going to do?"

"Go to college," Mama said automatically. I wonder if she ever wonders if that's true. "More coffee, Marion?"

"I'll get it, Mama." Honey leaped up, anxious to serve.

"That's okay, Honey. I was going out there anyway. I've got to check on the turkey."

If we followed Mama out to the kitchen we'd see her

refill Aunt Marion's pretty cup and her own with coffee and a splash of cream.

Then we'd see her set down the cups and go into her bathroom and open the medicine cabinet. She takes out an orange vial of pills and shakes one, no, two tablets into her palm, then gulps them down with a handful of water. Now she dries her lips and touches up her lipstick, smiles at herself in the mirror, stops smiling, applies more lipstick, smiles again, comes back into the kitchen, picks up the cups, and reappears.

"Here you go, Marion. I hope I gave you enough cream."

Why is Mama so afraid? Beneath her perpetual thirst for sleep is a terrible fear of waking.

The good thing about having so many people around is that they tend to dilute the brew. I didn't have to talk to Uncle Toddy; he watched football and charmed Gram and Gramps. They love him. Honey took off Gram's shoes and rubbed her feet, and told her what was new at school. Gram loves to have her feet rubbed. I don't do that anymore. The nails on her toes look like yellow shells.

Then we helped Uncle Toddy get dinner ready. We mashed potatoes and filled gravy boats. Uncle Toddy sliced open the turkey's breast. Honey clamored for the crispy golden skin.

I wrote the grace, but Honey said it. I wasn't in the mood to give thanks. I know I should; millions of people in the world are much worse off than I am. They're starving or buried alive in prison, cancer victims, and abused children, forgotten by God—Why doesn't He help them? I have plenty to eat and drink and wear, a warm place to sleep, and my family around me. So it could be worse, and I'm grateful it's not, but it probably will be. Amen.

The grace Honey gave was more traditional: "We thank thee, Lord, for bringing us together, and keeping this family safe from harm," etc. When she was finished, Grampa patted her hand and said, "Wonderful, Honey." He's a man of few words, but he means them. Grammy's eyes shone with love and pride. "That was just right, Honey," she said. "Thank you, dear."

Then we ate. Richie and the boys sat at a card table, watching the football game. Or perhaps it was a different game. Someone got hurt and was carried off the field while the crowd stood and cheered and the announcers agreed that they hoped he wouldn't be paralyzed forever.

After dinner we had Aunt Marion's homemade pies, which she presented with a flourish, like a magician. "We'll have these," she announced. "You can put the others back in the freezer."

A generous offer. But let's look closer: Put them *back in the freezer*—whence they came. Mama's pies weren't fresh and homemade; they were store-bought and frozen.

We'd thrown away the boxes. How did Aunt Marion know?

Gram and Gramps got tired and had to leave early. Grammy hugged me and said, "Pretty soon you'll be able to drive me." Grampa gave me a whiskery kiss. Richie helped them into their coats and took them home.

Honey played the piano. I made another pot of coffee. The men and boys played dominoes. Aunt Marion talked and Mama listened. At last it was time for our guests to go.

After they left we cleaned up the kitchen. Honey and Uncle Toddy did the dishes. She went *on* and *on* about what a terrific day it had been. I had to wonder: Where was I?

Richie helped Papa put away the chairs, then asked to use the car, but Papa said no. Our guests were gone and the show was over. My brother slammed the door on his way out.

I took some coffee to Mama, who was reading in bed.

"Aren't you sweet," she said, "but I'm falling asleep. Did you have a good time?"

"Yes. Did you?"

"Oh, yes," Mama said. "It was a lovely day." Her eyelids drooped, her book fell shut. "Now I'm so tired."

I'd given her coffee with caffeine all day. Which proves the power of the mind: Whatever you believe is true, is true, if you believe it.

Just when I think it won't happen again, when I think it was something I imagined, the ceiling above my head cracks open and my uncle descends like night.

My body can sense when it's going to happen. An electric current hums through the house.

I try to escape, spending the night with a friend. Sometimes the danger passes. But usually the house is still throbbing with his charge. It could explode any second. He could hurt somebody.

He comes not for Honey, but for me.

He frightened her so badly she couldn't breathe. She's weak. I protect my sister. When he comes I turn away from my eyes and walk down a long, dark hallway in my head, to the quiet place, where it's peaceful and safe.

I remain there until he's gone.

At dinner that night I read the signals with my skin. His eyeteeth lengthen imperceptibly.

"More linguine, Carolyn?"

"No, thanks. I'm stuffed. I was thinking I'd go over to Nancy's tonight, so we can study together, if that's all right."

"The linguine was delicious," Honey blurted, sensing waves ahead, trying to keep things smooth.

"I don't want you out tonight," Mama said. "It's cold."

"Richie could give me a ride."

Papa shook his head. "He's not using the car until he pulls himself together. We got a letter today from school."

"Carolyn, are you sure you don't want something else?"

"Positive, Uncle Toddy."

"I'll help Richie," Honey offered. "He's got plenty of time before the end of the semester."

I cleared away the plates. "I could walk to Nancy's."

"Not tonight," Papa said. "You heard your mother."

"Maybe Nancy could stay over."

"Not on a school night."

"I never get to do what I want!"

Honey cringed.

Mama looked shocked. "What's the matter with you, Carolyn?"

"It's my life, not yours!" My voice was shrill.

"I'll handle this, Doris. Go up to your room and stay there, young lady, until you're ready to apologize."

"Apologize for what?"

"For acting like a spoiled brat!"

"I'm not a brat! Nobody listens to me!"

My father stood up. Uncle Toddy said, "Bill."

"Get up there and stay there until you're ready to behave!" Papa shouted. Mama's eyes filled with tears.

I ran up the stairs to my bedroom and slammed the door. They hate it when I'm angry. Ladies don't get mad. No matter what they say, Honey never disagrees. I have to stay awake while she wraps herself in dreams.

I ignored her when she came in. She disgusts me.

I put on all the lights and tried to read, but my mind was listening to the noises in the house: creaks and taps and crunching sounds. I turned on the radio and exercised. I thought Honey might complain, but she kept sleeping.

The night dies slowly. The house is still. I mustn't fall asleep. He tries to surprise me.

I am reading the Bible Gram gave me when I made my first communion. My name is stamped in gold on the cover. Yea, though I walk through the Valley of the Shadow of Death, I will fear no evil for—

He is with me. The door opens. My uncle sticks his head into the room.

"I thought you'd fallen asleep with the lights on, Carrie."

He speaks softly so no one will hear him. Honey sleeps through this as she has so many times. For a moment I see him through her eyes: He's nice. Then his mask slides off. The eyes are bottomless, greedy.

"Get out," I say. "I'm going to sleep." I don't want to wake Honey. She wakes up screaming. I hold out my knife. "I'll kill you if you touch us." It's such a little knife, not fit for a vampire.

"Have you gone nuts? What's the matter with you?" He steps inside my room and shuts the door.

"You're killing us. You're drinking our blood."

"Are you crazy? I love you."

"He loves us to death."

Every muscle in my uncle's face turns down.

"Shut up," he says. "Are you on drugs? You're losing weight. You look terrible lately."

"I'm going to tell the police! I'll tell Mama and Papa!"

"Tell them what, that I'm drinking your blood?" He sits at the foot of my bed and regards me as if I'm an exotic bug he wants to inspect before he crushes it.

"Carolyn, do you hear what you're saying? Do you? People will think you're completely insane. And you are, if you believe that. Sweetie, listen to me."

He talks and talks. He begins to fill the room, the suffocating wings of his cape inflating.

"You were never like this. You've changed so much. It scares me, Carolyn, it really does. They'll take you away. And I couldn't stop them. We'd all be so sad. Your Grammy would die. And everybody would read about it in the newspaper and your dad would be mad. He wouldn't like that at all. But if you want me to, I'll call him right now, and you can tell him that I'm a vampire."

His face glistens with tears. They tremble on his lips. I watch them drop to the blanket, entranced.

"Why are you doing this to me, Carolyn? I would never hurt you. Have I ever hurt you?"

It doesn't matter what I answer. He doesn't listen. The knife and the Bible fall from my hands. He's not going to kill me. He craves a fix. He's addicted to my fear. There's lots to spare. Lots of blood. Lots of hair, long and thick and slippery. He loves to tangle his fingers in it, tightening his grip to hold me still.

The walls have collapsed and my bedroom is gone. I am trapped in the world that my uncle has made. No air, no light. The wind shrieks in my ears. His teeth nibble delicately at my neck, tenderizing the flesh that he will tear.

I have to get away. I have to escape. My eyes are open, but his face is gone. Inside my head, I have turned my back on him and am walking down a long dark hallway.

He can't hurt us now. Honey sleeps, safe. My family dreams while I keep walking. I leave my eyes behind and find the quiet place.

He clasps my throat like the neck of a bottle and drinks and drinks and drinks.

"For Thine is the kingdom, the power, and the glory. Forever and ever. Amen."

The prayer ends and I lift my head. Grammy smiles at me and squeezes my hand. Then we all stand and sing "Joy to the World." It's winter outside, but the church is warm and the altar is decorated with boughs of holly.

Holy little church! I feel so happy. My grandmother's voice is strong and true. She is an important part of the congregation because she has a kind heart. People love her. She's proud that I'm her granddaughter. I'm so glad she's my Grammy. She never holds back her love, like Mama and Papa do; no dessert until you finish your dinner. Grammy says, "No matter what, I'll always love you."

Promise me, Gram, that even when you're dead, you'll hold me in the arms of your love. I'm so scared and alone. Honey's acting strange and Richie has changed, and Maggie's gone so far away.

The service is over. Grammy smooths my hair, the most beautiful hair in the world, she tells me. "Shall we get some refreshments?"

"Oh, yes! I'm hungry!" Wonderful smells waft into the sanctuary.

We walk up the aisle past the gleaming pipe organ. The minister smiles and shakes our hands and welcomes us into the choir room, where the ladies are holding their Christmas bazaar.

The room's warm and cozy. I take off my sweater. It won't get lost; they'll know it's mine. Tables line the walls, covered with homemade items: slippers, dish towels, pot holders, fudge, baskets made of Christmas cards, and jars of brilliant jelly.

Down the hall other ladies are serving the bean supper. Grampa's in there, holding our places. But first I want to look at everything for sale.

I have money in my pocket for Christmas presents. Gram gave me money. Lots of money. I'm rich! I browse from table to table, and everybody smiles. Someone pins a tiny crocheted wreath on my blouse, free, because I'm me, and a child of this church, and my grandmother's precious flower.

The ladies behind the tables are big and soft. Their aprons are printed with Christmas bells. The room smells of cinnamon, vanilla, talcum powder. I feel happy and safe. The men are down the hall with Grampa, heaping their plates with franks and beans.

I buy a handkerchief embroidered with violets for Mama, a leather bookmark stamped with a cross for Papa, a pipe cleaner holder for Grampa.

But I can't find the right gift for Grammy. I look

and look. Nothing's good enough. I want to give her something perfect, something special.

She is suddenly beside me. "What's the matter, darling?"

"I want to give you something you'll love." I'm crying.

"I've got what I love." She puts her arms around me. Then she smiles in my face and dries my eyes. "There's no need to cry. This is a happy time. All better?" she asks.

I tell her I'm fine.

"Good," she says. "Let's go get some supper before your Grampa eats it all up."

She takes my hand and we walk down the hallway.

At the end of the hall is the front of my eyes. Gram and the ladies and the church are gone. My uncle's face comes into focus, wiping his lips on the back of his hand.

Honey and I have always suc-
ceeded at school, academi-
cally and, most importantly,
socially. The teachers think
they're in charge, but the
kids don't take them seriously. What matters is what
the other kids think, even if they're people you don't
like. It's odd.

No one bugs us because we're so popular. We're
pretty and smart. We've got a nice big house, a wonderful family, and our father drives a shiny new car. We're
invited to parties, we sing in the choir, and Honey
cheers our teams on to victory.

She's still cheering. I'm out of the play. My grades
were too bad. "You've got to cut back," the school
counselor said. "You're not taking care of business.
What's the problem, Carolyn?"

There is no problem. I didn't mind getting kicked
out of the play. The world is a stage. I'm always per-
forming.

Scene: In the fast-food place across from the high
school. A large group of attractive teens has comman-
deered the tables at the back of the restaurant. The boys
are big, and most wear jackets that indicate they're
jocks. Several of the girls wear cheerleading outfits:

blue-and-gold sweaters and short swirly skirts that brush their thighs.

Everyone is talking and laughing loudly. Honey is particularly animated because Bradley Curtis has given her a ring that she wears on a chain around her throat. It's his class ring, studded with a big red stone. It's getting all tangled up with her gold cross.

I guess that means they're going together. Whatever that means. He likes her a lot. She's sitting on his lap and ruffling his hair, talking about him as if they were married. She'd like that. Curtis Bradley is solid and strong. His family always makes her feel welcome. She's happy at his house; she never wants to come home.

I miss her, but I don't blame her.

I lean across the table to say something to Nancy, but it feels like I'm watching myself in a play. Maybe those are the stage directions: *I lean across the table to say something to Nancy.* We're making too much noise and the jukebox is playing and Nancy cups her ear and shouts: "What?"

The music is so loud I can feel it in my heart, the bass thumping *boom boom boom.* It's too noisy to talk. I say, "Ya ya ya ya ya!" Nancy laughs and says, "You're crazy!"

The door swings open; Annie Brown comes in with Janis Simms, the official school fat girl. They flinch when they see us and veer toward a table in the opposite direction. They're afraid that the boys will make jokes

about them. Glen Bond makes a typically unwitty re-
mark, and we all feel obliged to snicker.

Honey says, "Shut up," and gets off Bradley's lap and
crosses the room to Annie and Janis.

She makes small talk with them. Soon, they're laughing. Curtis watches her as if she's grown golden wings
to match her hair. If only he and Honey could fly away
and start a new life together. She would never run away.
Mama and Papa would be so hurt. She wants to please
people, kissing their hands, rolling onto her back like
a puppy. Don't kick me.

Honey leaves the girls smiling and comes back to
our table.

"You're so nice," Curtis tells her sincerely.

"She's a saint," I say.

Honey rolls her eyes and everybody laughs.

Scene: In the counselor's office. I stare intently at the
freckles on Ms. Johnson's face. If you connected all the
dots, what would they say?

". . . talked to you about this before." She's shuffling
papers on her cluttered desk. I highlight the word *clut-
ter* in my mind. It sounds like the object it describes.
What's the word? Onomono something.

". . . hasn't had much effect. Carolyn, I need your
cooperation. I can't do it by myself."

She's been talking for some time, I'm not sure how
long. I forgot to pay attention. Like when you ride

in a car and look out the window but your mind is somewhere else. So when you get where you're going, you can't remember the trip. Where does your mind go when it's not in your head?

"Carolyn!" Her hand is on my arm. Her look of concern is edged with irritation. "You're not listening to a word I'm saying."

"I'm sorry. I was just thinking."

"Thinking about what?"

"Nothing. Just a bunch of different things."

"Like what? Please tell me, Carolyn. I'm trying to help you."

"I appreciate your concern, but nothing's wrong," I say with such calm conviction that I almost believe it.

Ms. Johnson's eyes try to enter mine, but I've locked them. Then I throw away the key. Then I forget that the key existed. Then I forget that I forgot.

All of this only takes a second.

". . . lots of young people go through rebellious phases, but you've never been an average kid."

If she only knew. I almost crack up.

"Carolyn, I understand that you wouldn't feel comfortable 'telling on' Richie, but we're very concerned. About both of you. I've tried to contact your parents. I've talked to your uncle several times, and he tells me he's given your mother the message."

"Mama hasn't been well."

"I'm sorry to hear that. Nothing serious, I hope."

"She's depressed."

I can't believe that I've told the truth and not given the official family explanation: She's tired. No one ever says what's wrong with Mama, but the implication is that it's a medical condition. Like sleeping sickness; not something in her mind but in her body. But if her mind is ill, then her body will be too, because you can't have one without the other. No matter what you do, you can't escape yourself. Everywhere you go, there you are.

". . . so thin. Have you thought about seeing your family doctor? I know you girls like to be nice and skinny, but there's a limit, Carolyn."

Really? Where is it? I think I've crossed it. What's happening to me? Why am I in this office? My uncle's been a vampire since I was little. Why is my life disintegrating now? Is he taking so much blood that he's draining my brain? I want to close my eyes. I am so exhausted. I stayed awake last night. I heard the floorboards creaking, or mice squeaking. The mice are worse; the house is full of tiny turds.

". . . this essay. Mrs. Bennett found it very disturbing." Ms. Johnson is holding up a sheaf of papers. "You were supposed to write about *To Kill a Mockingbird*."

She hands me the papers, and I glance at the title in the center of the first page: "Does Evil Exist?" The essay runs to ten typed pages. I don't remember writing it.

My eyes sweep the pages, looking for something familiar. The sentences are coherent, but foreign. "Is evil another face of God's?" "Is free choice a cross or a key to the kingdom of heaven?" "Babies are born guilt-less into a world that is ancient with sin."

What have I written? Have I betrayed myself? No, it's just me, going on and on about the sorrow and suffering in the world, etc. Just me, losing my mind on paper.

"I was exploring the immorality of racism," I say, "which, as you know, is the theme of the book. I exam-ined the struggle between good and greed, which are the two dominating forces in the world."

Ms. Johnson's eyes are troubled, and she's very smart. But once again I have fooled her. I keep waiting for her to ask the right questions so I can tell the truth. But then she might say: "Go away, you're crazy!" She would scrub her office clean with holy water.

She says, "I guess Mrs. Bennett didn't see the connec-tion."

"That's how I read the book," I say. "Maybe I was being too subtle."

I hate to lie to those honest eyes. You can see clear through them to her heart. But there's nothing to say. I can't talk about Richie. I can't talk about myself or Honey. I love my mama. I love my Grammy. I don't want to hurt them. I'd rather die.

*   *   *

Scene: The front porch of the family home. The sun is setting and the sky is purple. Richie is sitting on the steps, smoking a cigarette. It's cold, but he doesn't want to go inside because he and my father will get into a fight. It happens every night, like dinner.

"You shouldn't smoke those," I tell him.

"Don't start," he says. Does he mean Don't start smoking or Mind your own business?

"Ms. Johnson is worried about you," I say. "She called me in today."

"What did you tell her?"

"I didn't tell her anything. What are you doing? Are you selling drugs?"

He laughs. "Is that what they're saying?"

"Some people are. You could get in trouble."

"Trouble's my middle name." A joke. His middle name is Walter. "No, I'm not selling drugs. Just take it easy." He speaks gently because he loves me. Underneath, he's still Richie, who used to be my brother.

"I'm worried about you," I say.

"Things are under control. Just take care of yourself. That's the thing to do. Everybody's on their own."

"We're supposed to be a family."

"But we're not." He shrugs. "It's not my fault it's a drag."

"Papa says you're flunking, you won't graduate."

"That's my problem, not his." He lights another cigarette, its tip glows red. "I'll tell you one thing, come June, I'm gone. I'm out of here."

"No! Richie, please don't go away!"

"I'll be around," he says. "It's not like I'll disappear. You better go inside. You're shivering."

"I wanted to talk to you. We never talk anymore."

"We're talking right now. Come on, you're freezing." He takes my hand and tugs me toward the door.

We almost make it through dinner without a scene; then Papa says he doesn't like Richie's attitude and Richie says he doesn't like Papa's either. Papa slaps his face and Richie almost slugs him, but Uncle Toddy jumps between them. He's such a great guy.

Curtain.

I waved frantically when I saw Maggie at the station, scanning the windows of the train. She shouted something I couldn't hear; the train was coming to a stop.

I stumbled down the stairs and into her arms.

"Look at you!" she shrieked. "I can't believe it! You're actually here! This is great!"

Porters and passengers swirled around us. We hugged and danced.

"I can't believe they let you come!"

"They almost didn't. I couldn't believe it myself, till I was on the train."

"Don't they feed you, or what? You're so skinny!" she cried. "How much do you weigh?"

"I don't know. A hundred and five."

"Each of my thighs weighs a hundred and five! I'll donate some fat in your name."

I basked in her warmth; in the intelligent eyes, in the curly brown poodle hair framing her face.

We collected my luggage. "The car's over there. It's Michael's, don't you love it?" It was a red VW. "He can't wait to meet you."

"I thought he might be here."

"I wanted you all to myself for a while. He's coming

for dinner tomorrow night." Maggie stuffed my suit-cases into the backseat. "What's in these things? I can barely lift them. I invited you for Christmas, not the rest of your life."

"Oh," I said. "I thought you wanted to adopt me."

Maybe I could go to Boston University; not live with Maggie, but somewhere close. We could cook spaghetti feasts and go shopping together. *I was just in the neigh-borhood so I thought I'd drop by.* . . . *"Oh, hi!" Maggie would say. "Come on in!"*

Soon we were zipping through heavy traffic. Maggie navigated down narrow streets, finally parking in front of an old brick house.

"Good news," she said. "We're on the second floor."

We lugged my suitcases up the stairs, Maggie pre-tending she was going to collapse. She unlocked her apartment, and I felt instantly at ease; this was where I had pictured my sister.

The apartment was large and full of afternoon light. The floors were covered with braided rugs. The furni-ture was old and comfortable-looking. Two blue para-keets in a cage near the window burst into song as we entered the room.

"It's wonderful, Maggie! Where is everybody?"

"Away for Christmas vacation. We have the place to ourselves. Put your bags in here. You're staying in Trudy's room."

"Are you sure she doesn't mind? Could I have her boyfriend too?" I admired a framed photograph on her nightstand.

"Sorry. They're engaged. I wish you could meet her. And Rachel and Linda. They've heard me talk about you for years. They feel like they already know you."

"I feel like I know them too." There's a picture of the four of them on my bulletin board at home; a joyous chorus line, kicking their legs.

"We get along so well, it's amazing," Maggie said. "They're just like family. It's incredible. I didn't realize people could live in the same house and still like each other. You know what I mean; things get tense at home. But here, it's funny. We get along great. Come on, I'll show you the rest of the place. You can unpack later."

There were three other bedrooms and one tiny bathroom.

"That's where the fights break out," Maggie said. "Things get a little frantic in the morning." The kitchen was small, but there were plenty of cupboards, which Maggie said was handy because they kept most of their food separate.

"Otherwise, it's like: 'Who ate my granola bars? Who finished the chocolate chips?' And nobody cops to the crime and we have to dust for prints. Some stuff we share, like when we have a big dinner. Then everybody pitches in."

"Like Thanksgiving," I said, remembering the laughter I'd heard over the telephone. "It sounded like you guys were having a great time."

"Oh, we did!" Maggie glowed. "Michael and David, that's Trudy's boyfriend, were chasing each other with this frozen turkey! We laughed so hard. Sit down and relax! Would you like some tea or coffee or juice?"

"Coffee, please, with lots of caffeine. I'm having a sinking spell."

"Rough trip?"

"It was okay. Just long."

"You should've flown."

"No way. You know how I feel about planes."

I sat on the living room rug, leaning against a big pillow. It would've felt good to close my eyes. But I didn't want to waste a moment with my sister.

On the mantel over the fireplace was a picture of me and Maggie, playing dress up, in Grammy's old clothes. We stared unsmiling into the camera. Make-believe was serious business. It made me happy to see that picture. Everyone who came to the apartment would know that Maggie and I were close. There were pictures of me in her bedroom too, which was as tidy as her room had been at home.

"How was the food on the train?" she called from the kitchen.

"Lousy. But who felt like eating? My stomach felt queasy. But the scenery was great."

"I still can't believe you're really here. Did you threaten them or something?"

"Actually, yes. I told them I'd kill myself if they made me stay home for Christmas."

"How merry of you! Be careful, this is hot." Maggie handed me a mug of coffee and cream.

"God, that's good. You make the best coffee."

"Some people think it's too strong."

"Wimps."

"Exactly." Maggie brought out a plate of brownies. "Got to fatten you up. As you can see, that's not my problem. But who has time to obsess about weight? I like the way I look, and Michael does too. Who cares what people think? Well, you do, obviously. I mean it, Carrie, you're too skinny."

Maggie wasn't fat or even pudgy; just soft where she'd been sharp.

She patted my leg. "It's so good to see you. I never thought they'd let you come."

"They didn't want to. But I was so bummed out they got worried. They thought the trip might cheer me up. And it did. I'm cured! It's a miracle!"

"And Papa didn't have a fit about the cost? Or is he taking it out of your allowance forever?"

"Let's just say he wasn't thrilled. But Uncle Toddy convinced him that it was cheaper than the alternative."

"What alternative?" Maggie bit into a brownie.

"A brain transplant."

"No, seriously."

"I don't know. A shrink, I guess."

"Are you kidding? I can't tell." Maggie peered into my face. "Why were you so bummed out?"

I waved away the questions. "Let's not talk about that now. Once I got on the train, I felt great. Nauseous, but great. Jeez, you wouldn't believe some of the passengers! Some of them were pretty squirrely. The old lady sitting beside me had on nylons that came up to her shins."

"Great look," Maggie said. "Let's never get old."

"She was reading this romance novel with teeny little print. Just the *thought* of reading made me sick."

"I could never read in the car. Richie could, remember? He'd sit there with those books by that science fiction guy, what was his name?"

"Piers Anthony." Richie used to be his biggest fan. I haven't seen him read a book in ages.

"How's Mama doing?"

I took another sip of creamy coffee. "The good news is, she doesn't feel too bad. The bad news is, she doesn't feel too good."

"Is she still on medication?"

"Let's not talk about them now. I promise I'll go into all that later. I escaped! I'm free! They're far away! I love it here! Won't you please adopt me?"

Maggie laughed. She thought I was kidding.

* * *

Christmas with Maggie was a dream come true, and I owed it all to Uncle Toddy. When I begged my parents to let me go to Massachusetts, they reacted as if I'd asked to fly to the moon: Don't be absurd. It's too far away. It's too expensive. Anyway, maybe Maggie would come home next summer.

"Next summer will be too late!" I'd cried.

Papa said, "Don't be melodramatic."

Uncle Toddy knew I wasn't acting. "Let her go," he said. "The change will do her good. She misses her big sister."

"I can't afford it," Papa said. Is that really true? He and Mama are planning a cruise to Bermuda. It's part of their upcoming anniversary gala, when they will celebrate twenty-five years of holy gridlock. Wedlock, I mean. To keep romance in a marriage, it's important to take time away from the kids, particularly if you can't stand them.

Uncle Toddy will be in charge while they're gone.

He paid for half of my train ticket.

"Do you feel like going for a ride?" Maggie asked. "Or do you want to hang around? It's up to you."

"Let's go for a ride."

"We can stop by and say hi to Michael. He works at the campus bookstore. God, your hair is beautiful."

I had unbound my braid and was brushing it out.

"I'm thinking of cutting it off."

"Why?"

"It gets tangled up. I'm tired of it."

"Then give it to me."

"All right," I said. "I'll leave it to you in my will."

We left the apartment and cruised toward the campus.

"We'll just run in so you can say hi to Michael. I'm curious to see what you think of him. He's so wonderful! Well, that's my opinion!"

"Maggie, are you going to marry him?"

She stopped at a traffic light and scrunched up her nose. "Gee, I've never considered it."

"You lie!" I poked her in the ribs, and she accidentally honked the horn.

"Now that you mention it, it's crossed my mind. Five or six million times. Actually, we're talking about it. I love him, Carrie, I really do. And he loves me. Isn't that a handy arrangement?"

I'm surprised that the whole world's not in love with Maggie. It felt so good to laugh with my sister. The tension and fear that had gripped me let go. I felt content and infinitely calm.

Michael crossed the bookstore to us, holding out his hand.

"Carrie," he said, "it's so nice to meet you! Maggie talks about you all the time."

He wasn't handsome, but he had a good face, a face

you could look at for the rest of your life, a face that would never lie.

"Maggie talks about you all the time too," I said. "Let's face it: Maggie talks all the time."

We laughed. His arm rested lightly on her shoulders. He looked so pleasant and tall and strong. He showed me around the bookstore briefly. Then Maggie and I drove to a park.

It was almost dark. Old-fashioned lamps were draped with Christmas garlands. Bundled-up children skated on a frozen pond while carols blared from a loudspeaker.

"It's beautiful here in the spring," Maggie said, "when all the trees are in blossom. You can go out on the lake in the swan boats."

"It's beautiful now. I love Boston."

"I knew you would. It's your kind of town; full of bookstores and interesting shops, and not so big that it swallows you up. I could always picture you here."

"And now I'm here." I never wanted to go home again.

We drove around, admiring the Christmas lights and decorations, the displays of plastic crèches and candy canes and Santas.

Maggie said, "Remember when the folks admitted Santa wasn't real?"

"Remember it? I'm still not over it."

"Yeah," Maggie said. "You took it hard."

"Well, why did they lie? I kept asking them about it: Is there really a Santa? And they always said yes, and if you don't believe in him, he won't bring you any presents. Then one day it's like: Forget what we said. We were just pretending. After that, I never trusted them again."

"Aren't you being a little harsh? I mean, they weren't trying to swindle you. They just wanted you to believe in Santa Claus."

"Why?"

"Because it's fun to believe."

"Not when it's a lie. I'd never do something like that to my kids."

Maggie started to joke, but then she saw that I was serious.

Maggie worked as a waitress in a busy restaurant. She managed to get time off from her job.

"It's crazy there at Christmas, with the shoppers," she said, "but I told Frank, my boss, my sister was visiting, and he said fine. He's really nice."

We'd wake up in the mornings and eat a big breakfast. "We've got to put some weight on you, girl," Maggie said, loading my plate with honeyed toast and scrambled eggs.

Then we'd shop for Christmas presents or admire the displays in store windows, or visit a museum or a beautiful old church. One day we drove out into the country. Snow was piled high on either side of the highway. We cut down a fir at a tree farm, then tied it to the ski rack on Michael's car. He helped us decorate the tree after dinner. He came over after work almost every night, bringing loaves of crusty French bread and bottles of wine, or pastries made of raspberries and chocolate. It was easy to see how much he and Maggie loved each other. I prayed that Michael would never go away.

On Christmas Day we opened our presents. Maggie knew what would please me: a journal covered in Chinese silk, paperback books, warm socks, beaded earrings. When our family called, I hid in the shower. I didn't want to talk to my parents or wish Uncle Toddy a merry Christmas. I wanted all of them to leave me alone.

"She's doing fine," I heard Maggie say. "We're having a great time. I know she'll be sorry she missed you."

We shared Christmas dinner with friends of Maggie and Michael, who were married and had two-year-old twins. Other friends dropped by to drink eggnog and sing carols. I sat on the floor and played with the kids. "She's so good with the twins," I heard their mother tell Maggie. I'd never had such a wonderful Christmas.

Soon it would be time to return to California. I didn't

want to leave my sister. I needed to ask her if she'd ever experienced what I'd experienced. I needed to hear her say I wasn't crazy.

When my parents called to tell me they'd meet my train, I hid in the bathroom again.

"You have to talk to them sometime," Maggie said. "They're beginning to wonder if you're really here."

"Maggie, you don't know what it's like there," I said. "Things have gotten a lot worse since you left."

"What do you mean?" She was curled up on the sofa, a quilt over her legs. Logs snapped and crackled in the fireplace.

"Maggie, did you ever notice anything strange about Uncle Toddy?"

"Strange? Like what? Like he can't hold a job? Like, he never brings his girlfriends home? Like, no matter how old he gets, he still looks young? Little things like that?"

"Well, kind of. Not exactly. It's just that, this is kind of hard to explain. You know how Mama always seems depressed?"

"Really? Yes, now that you mention it."

"I'm serious, Maggie. You can't talk to her anymore. She doesn't want to be upset. And Papa's just as bad."

Maggie nodded her head. "You can't talk to Papa. He doesn't know how to listen. Before you even stop talking, he's disagreeing. That's always driven me insane."

"Well, see, they're pretty worked up lately because

Richie's going down the drain. I mean, I didn't want to bring this up before, because we were having such a nice Christmas. But I'm scared, Maggie. I'm really worried. He's changed. He's really skinny."

"You don't look so hot yourself. Will you calm down? You're practically hyperventilating."

I was pacing around the room. "I don't know what to do. Honey always says to make the best of everything. But how do you make the best of someone drinking your blood?"

"Whoa, slow down. You lost me there. What are you talking about? Will you please sit down?"

"I can't, I'm too nervous. You'll think I'm crazy." I knelt on the floor beside the sofa and let my hair fall forward to cover my face.

"I'd never think you're crazy. No matter how nutty you are," Maggie said. "I'm joking! Don't look at me like that. I was kidding. Carrie, listen to me. No matter what's wrong, you can tell me."

"Are you sure you won't think I'm crazy?"

"I promise. Carrie, I'm your sister. I love you. I'll help you." She gently stroked my hair. "You don't have to be scared. No one's ever going to hurt you again. In fact, I've been thinking. I wanted to surprise you. Carrie, I want you to live with me. You can share my room until we get our own place."

I lifted my face, my heart soaring. "What about Michael?"

"We've already discussed this. He knows how hard it's been for you lately. He thinks you should stay with us. We'll get a big place, or a house with a guest cottage, so you can be close but we'll have our own space. How does that sound?"

"It sounds wonderful!" I hugged her. "Oh, Maggie, I love you. I don't want to butt in on you and Michael. I just want to be close to you. That would be perfect! But what about the folks? They'll never let me stay. They'll say I'm too young to move out here."

"Don't worry, I've already talked to them about it. At first Papa was pretty upset. And Mama cried. Well, she always cries. But then they said—" Maggie paused and frowned. "Carrie, what's that man saying?"

"What man?"

"That man who's talking to you."

I look up to where she's pointing. Mr. Jepson, my science teacher, is standing beside my desk. He's very angry.

Everyone in class is staring at us. He's waving my science folder in my face. He's waving away Maggie.

He says: "What's the matter with you, Carolyn? This folder is empty. You told me you'd complete the missing assignments over Christmas vacation."

I say, "I'm sorry, Mr. Jepson. I went away."

If the TV had been working, maybe nothing would have happened. Little things can make a big difference. Life is full of close calls where you almost got killed but you left the house one min-ute later so the car that would've hit you missed you instead. Or the shots fired at random chose another innocent victim.

The TV wasn't working, and the house was too quiet. We were trapped at the dinner table like shipwreck survivors, clinging to a raft while the sun burned our bones.

Papa tried to make the TV work, but it was finished.

Uncle Toddy said, "It's been acting flaky."

Papa kept twirling knobs and pushing buttons. "Maybe there's a problem with the remote," he said, prying open the wand. The batteries fell out.

Mama said, "Bill, come eat your dinner."

"Do you mind? I want to see the news. I've got news for you, people: There's a world out there."

Papa had had too many drinks before dinner. He crouched down and examined the back of the set.

"Don't mess around with that," Uncle Toddy said. "It says right on it—"

"—to call a technician. Yes, I can read." Papa lost

his balance and landed on his butt, and Richie laughed. Papa snarled: "You think that's funny?" Richie said: "I'm laughing with you, not at you." Papa said, "I'm not laughing!"

Honey sensed the life raft drifting into dangerous waters.

"Papa, there's news on the radio," she said. "I'll go get mine. You can use it."

"That's swell," Papa said, "but the picture is terrible."

She shriveled like a whipped dog. Don't hurt me.

"She was just trying to help!" Richie threw down his fork.

"Relax, everybody." Uncle Toddy's voice was smooth. "I slave all day over a hot microwave. The least you people can do is have the decency to eat this delicious dinner. Come sit down, Bill."

"Go ahead. I'll be right there."

Mama sighed. And because the TV set wasn't filling the room with sports scores or weather reports, her sigh exploded in the silence.

I realized I'd heard that sigh all my life, as constant and familiar as my own breathing. It is the wind in the tree outside my bedroom window. A wind full of rain and storms.

"Mmm," Honey said, "the chicken looks fabulous."

What a trooper she is! That kid's got spunk! Sharks are circling the life raft and she's looking on the bright side, which happens to be the sun reflecting off their teeth.

"It smells delicious, Uncle Toddy." She held out her plate.

I asked Richie how things were going at school.

He snorted and rolled his eyes.

Meanwhile, Papa was playing with the TV set. "God-damn thing, it's only three years old. You pay a lot of money and what do you get? Junk."

Uncle Toddy said, "Didn't you get the extended warranty?"

Papa loomed up beside the table like a whale. There he blows. "That's the thing that really pisses me off! You're standing there, ready to buy the damn thing, and the salesman says, 'Do you want the extended warranty?' And of course that's fifty bucks extra. But *he* knows and *you* know that the thing's going to break down. That's the only guarantee you're going to get. It's going to break down, as soon as you get home, if you don't pay the fifty bucks extra. I mean what's happening to this country? What's happened to our pride? Let's just come right out and admit it: The whole damn thing is going down the tubes!"

When the TV is working, there's little conversation. If you start to talk, Papa says: "Wait, I want to hear this."

We didn't always have the TV on during dinner. It

began four, maybe five years ago, during some kind of international crisis, a war or hostages or something. Papa was furious and had to watch every minute. He kind of liked it; it took his mind off his problems. And then it got to be a habit, with various newscasters our nightly dinner guests.

"Bill," Uncle Toddy drawled, "your dinner's getting frozen."

"In a minute," Papa called from the den. We could hear him yanking open the file cabinet drawers. Later, Honey would go in there and clean up his mess. Look, Papa: The elves were here again!

"Honey," Mama said, "Bradley called this afternoon. I forgot to tell you. He wants you to call him tonight."

"Okay, Mama." She was wolfing down her dinner as if she hadn't eaten for a week. Maybe she hadn't. She's looking shabby lately. Her lips are dry and cracked.

I looked around the table and really saw my family. When the TV's on, we hide in the noise. The silence shone on us like a spotlight, stripping us of our shadows.

Mama was beautiful but dry and brittle, like a flower pressed in a book long ago.

My brother was the color of the milk he wasn't drinking. His skin was waxy. He was picking the skin off his chicken.

Uncle Toddy was a beacon of health. His body was

tough and slender. He's been lifting weights; he's been working out. At night his barbells thump the floor.

Honey's neck had been chewed like the bones on her plate. Her blouse clearly framed the hickeys, red mouths crying out. But nobody said: *By the way, have you been dating a werewolf lately?* Mama asked Honey about a basketball game. Honey poured on the pep: That game was so great! Richie's eyes rolled until his sockets were white, as if he were blind, which is what he wishes.

I saw everything clearly, an eye in the sky, as objective as God, and as far away.

My father gave up on finding the warranty, or forgot what he was looking for, and came back to the table. He seemed to notice the bruises on Honey's neck, and I thought: This is it!

But he sat down and ate his dinner. If Honey came to the table with an axe in her head, would he say, "Hon, your part is crooked"?

Looking around the table I almost laughed. You laugh or you cry until your guts pour out and you're inside out and the pain of it kills you. What a family! We're afraid that if we open our mouths the truth will jump out and ignite the air and the house will burst into flames. Instead, it smolders.

I wondered about those bruises on Honey's neck. There were two possibilities: Bradley Curtis or Uncle

Vampire. If Uncle Toddy had attacked her, Honey's scream would have awakened me. Unless I was too exhausted. I can't stay awake every minute of my life.

"And there's cobbler for dessert," my uncle announced.

My mother looked at him as if he'd burst into song. It took a minute for her brain to decode the message. She lives in her head, not in this house.

Then she perked up and described her day, in detail. We were with her as she curled and mascaraed each lash; as she toured the produce aisle at the supermarket and personally selected each banana.

Papa tossed Uncle Toddy the brochure for the cruise. "You see this? It shows the ship and the island."

Uncle Toddy examined the colorful pamphlet. It was full of photographs of people swimming, fishing, water-skiing, smiling.

"They say the food on these cruises is unbelievable," Uncle Toddy said. "You better figure on gaining five pounds."

"It better be good, at these prices," Papa said.

Honey looked at the brochure too, but Richie didn't take it.

Papa was talking about the trip. I was having trouble listening. Something about the words frightened me away.

"—for a week, but I figured it would take her that long to relax."

"Stay as long as you like," Uncle Toddy said.

"How long are you going to be gone?" I asked.

"Two weeks," Papa said. "Weren't you listening?"

"Two weeks?"

"Don't worry," Uncle Toddy said. "We'll be fine."

I started to speak, but Honey cut me off and blabbed some more about the fabulous dinner. Uncle Toddy ate up every word.

He will drink my blood, drink every drop. It is never enough, he is always thirsty. When they return from their trip, it will be too late to save me. I'll be nothing but bones and hair.

After dessert Honey went into the den and picked up the files lying on the floor. Uncle Toddy said he'd see about the TV set tomorrow.

"It might be cheaper to get a new one," he said.

"Whatever," Papa said, reading the newspaper.

I did the dishes. Then I went upstairs to the bathroom and locked the door. The white tile was so bright it burned my eyes. A shining clean mirror covered one wall. I turned on the radio Richie keeps in there. Wherever he is, he has to have noise. Silence can be scary; you can hear your heart beating, you can hear what your mind is thinking. You think about stuff that makes you sad, like hungry dogs lost on city streets, and kids who get abused and they're crying and crying. There's no use thinking about things you can't fix, so it's better not to have those pictures in your mind. I pray to God. I say, Dear God, why do you let this bad stuff happen? Grammy says it's not His fault; that the devil is strong because lots of people give him their power. They choose evil over good, and wrong over right. But little children get hurt, and they never had a choice. They come into this world and get hit in the face, and it makes me sick. It makes me wish I wasn't alive. Especially when I'm down. So if you put on the radio sometimes it helps drown out the sad thoughts in your mind.

I opened the medicine cabinet and took out the scissors. My bangs needed trimming. I snipped and snipped. The next thing I knew, I had cut off half my hair. A golden flag was lying on the floor. The girl in the mirror smiled calmly at me. The hair on one side of her head was long; on the other side, it was stubble.

Once that was done I had to keep cutting, because you can't go around split down the middle. The hair slid from the scissors and fell to the floor. My white scalp gleamed through the bristles.

The radio cheered me up. The deejay chattered. The stuff he said was supposed to be funny. Listening, I thought: I take life too seriously. Everything changes. Hair grows back. I kept snipping and snipping. My hair was so thick. It hadn't been cut since I was little. I felt light and free. My head turned easily from side to side. Framed in the mirror I saw someone new, a solitary seed breaking through the ground.

Honey was going to kill me.

Her reaction was almost comical. She stared at my reflection in the bathroom mirror as if I were a monster from hell.

"I can't believe this! How could you do this?" She reacted just as I'd expected. Honey is always the star of the show. The rest of us are scenery. "You're insane. Why didn't you just cut off your head and make everybody happy? You're such a freak!"

"Oh, go hide in your piano."

"I don't want to be seen with you! This is so embarrassing! You might as well wear a clown costume to school!"

"Fine. Can I borrow your cheerleading outfit?"

"You're out of control. You've gone over the edge. I mean, look at you!"

"Did you hear what they said at the table tonight? They're going away for two weeks!"

"So?"

"So look at your neck! He's drinking our blood! He's going to kill us!"

Honey laughed harshly. "Keep that up and they'll put you away."

"Where did the marks come from?"

"Duhhh. Let me think. Let's see if we can figure it out."

"Bradley did that?"

"As if you didn't know. You're jealous because he

loves me. Nobody loves you. You're such a pervert. It's disgusting."

She sounded vicious. She didn't sound like Honey.

"Who's that?"

"Who's who?"

"You're not acting like you. You're acting like someone else."

"Oh, God." She smirked. She shook her head. "You're as crazy as they say you are."

"Who says I'm crazy?"

"Everybody does! Just take a good look in the mirror!"

Richie knocked at the door.

"Just a minute, Rich."

"That's okay, I'll go downstairs."

"Richie, wait." I stuck my head out the door.

He came back down the hall, his eyes wide with amazement. He said, "Man, when you go, you go all the way."

"Does it look too awful?"

"Not exactly." He grinned. "But I want to be there when you show the folks. We better have an ambulance standing by."

"They like my hair better than me," I said.

"They'll probably keep your hair and kick you out."

"I'll be downstairs in a few minutes." I closed the door. "He doesn't think it looks bad," I told Honey.

"He's your brother. What did you expect him to say? If you wanted to change it, you should've gone to a salon. It looks like you cut it with your teeth," Honey said.

When I came into the living room Richie was hanging around, waiting for the show to start. My mother saw me, stood up, and put her hands to her heart, like a heroine in a horror movie.

"My God!" she cried. "What have you done to yourself?"

My father put down his newspaper. "Jesus Christ! Have you lost you mind?"

"No."

"You look like hell. I can't believe you'd do this. Are the other kids cutting their hair? Is that it? I thought you were a leader, not a follower, Carolyn." My father was as furious as if I'd cut off his hair. Uncle Toddy stared at me but didn't speak.

"I just felt like cutting it."

"Oh, Carolyn," Mama sighed. "Why would you want to make yourself look ugly?"

"I don't look ugly." I hoped I looked hideous. I hoped they would turn away and leave me alone.

"You can't go to school like that," Mama said. "You'll have to wear something on your head."

"I've got a Dodgers hat she can use."

"Be quiet, Rich. This isn't funny," Papa said.

"I'm disappointed in you, Carolyn. I didn't think you were so stupid. You've ruined yourself. You look terrible."

My uncle said, "I think she looks beautiful."

The hair on my head is long and golden. It drips down the stairs like gasoline, trickling into every room, then down into the cellar.

"Such beautiful hair," my uncle whispers.

It's a snare, a thicket. Bats get in it. They get caught in your hair and you can't get them out.

"Cut it out, Richie."

He's laughing at me. He says, "Why didn't you just cut off your head? What are you trying to tell me?"

Why not? I thought. I should cut off my head. Everything would be so quiet.

"What an actress! Such a prima donna!" Honey's voice is rough. She's tired of me. "Get lost," she tells me. "Get a life."

"No, don't go. Don't leave me," I beg.

You know I can't live without you.

My uncle loves me. Even though I'm crazy. My parents hate me. They are so disappointed. I am ruining the portrait of our perfect family. They wish Richie and I would go away. They wish I would be like Honey. A good girl always obeys adults. No matter how nuts they are.

It's enough to drive a person crazy.

* * *

I'm lost in the forest, in the middle of the night, with a handful of bread crumbs to eat when I get hungry, or to mark my path, so I can find my way out.

I'm starving.

Honey says: "Don't let it smell the yeast on your breath. It feeds on living things."

I know what she means. I've seen the beast. He tails me like a shadow. Can you see him? There, in the corner of your eye? He rushes toward you—

Grab the knife beneath your pillow, it's a butcher knife now, long and gleaming. Swing at the thing with all your might, chopping, hacking, slashing off an arm. Slash off the other arm. Blood pours out.

But the thing keeps coming. Chasing you.

Turn and slash, the knife blade flashes; no head, no legs. You can't escape. A bloody stump now, the thing keeps coming. It knows where you're hiding. It finds you.

Honey waves a white flag out the window. No, it's the banner of her moonlit hair. She leans out too far, her legs fly up. I try to grab her, she slips through my fingers. She plunges down. The ground inhales her.

"Wake up," Maggie says. "You're having a dream."

"How can you tell if it's a dream?" I ask her.

Maggie taps a pointer on the blackboard. "There are two ways to tell if you're dead or dreaming. I've written them on the blackboard so you can copy them down."

I take out my journal and a pen. "I'm ready."

"If you're dreaming, you can wake up and make toast," Maggie says. "But if you're dead, you can't taste it."

I try to follow what she's saying. Smoke fills my nose.

"That's because the house is burning." My uncle's voice is like a finger in my ear. He startles me so badly I jump out of my skin and am beside myself. I pull myself together, trembling.

"Where did you come from?"

"I'm always around." He buffs his silver claws on his cape.

My closed bedroom door is outlined in pulsing light. "Don't open that," he says.

I fling open the door. Every room downstairs is orange, blazing. I see that my long golden hair is the fuse. It clears the top step of the stairs and crackles toward me.

"Don't be scared. You won't get hurt." He licks his lips. He's hungry.

I say: "If you touch me, I'll kill you."

"You can't," he says. "We're already dead."

I run to the window and crash through the glass. My uncle lunges for me and misses. I'm falling through darkness in a shower of slivers.

"Catch me, Grammy!"

She looks up and sees me, her face lit like the moon. She reaches out her frail arms. They're trembling. "I'll try," she cries, "but I'm an old lady."

Hurtling through darkness, I realize in that instant that if I land on my grandmother, I will kill her.

Nancy said, "You need to talk to someone."

We were standing outside the gym after school. She had brought along Bradley Curtis for backup.

"Talk to who?" I said.

They studied the ground. If they had looked in my eyes, they would've seen me there, hiding. I have abandoned my feet, my fingers, my body. I am watching from the top floor. The house is blazing.

"A doctor or someone. Maybe Ms. Johnson. It just seems like you're not happy or something."

"I'm okay."

"You seem so different."

"My hair, you mean."

"Yeah!" Bradley said, then grimaced. He hadn't meant to shout. He's uncomfortable with me when Honey's not around.

"People like my hair." Oddly, this was true. At first people were shocked, but later that week other girls came to school with their hair chopped off. When you're popular, people think you know what you're doing.

"It's not just your hair; it's everything," Nancy said.

Some people went by. We all said hi, smiled and said hi hi hi hi hi.

"You don't seem like you," she said. "Why won't you

tell me what's wrong? Did I do something to you? Don't you trust me anymore?"

There were tears in her eyes. Nancy was in pain. I'd hurt her, and she was not to blame for anything.

"Of course I trust you. Don't you believe me? I'm telling you, everything's fine."

Nancy looked as if I'd slapped her. Curtis Bradley plunged his hands into his pockets, hunching his shoulders around his ears as if the sound of my voice were torture.

"We care about you a lot." He sounded stiff and formal.

"Gee, thanks!" I said. Bradley Curtis winced.

They're doing this for Honey's sake. I've become an embarrassment to her. A disgrace. Everybody loves Honey. Even I love Honey. The Princess of Perfection. The Queen of Pretend.

We stood there, not speaking. Curtis Bradley looked sick.

"I really do appreciate your concern," I said. "But there's nothing wrong. Really, I'm fine."

They backed off, Nancy hugging her books as if shielding her heart from my face.

I watched them cross the campus to Nancy's car. They turned and looked back at me. I waved as they drove away.

I appreciate their concern, I really do, but everything

is under control. Yesterday I decided to talk to the school counselor. There is no place else left for me to go.

I don't know why I didn't tell them that. The habit of secrecy is hard to break, even when the season for secrets is over.

I have an appointment to talk to Ms. Johnson today.

I began to cross the campus to her office.

Yesterday afternoon she'd stopped me in the halls and said, "Carolyn, we've got to talk about your grades. This is serious."

I was too tired to resist. "All right," I said, knowing the fight would come later, with my sister.

Ms. Johnson looked relieved. "After school today?"

"Tomorrow afternoon would be better."

I needed to tell Honey what I was going to do. I asked her to go with me.

Honey was enraged. "Have you lost your mind? You can't talk to Ms. Johnson! What's the matter with you?"

"I can't stand it anymore."

"There's nothing to stand! You've made up the whole damn thing in your head!"

"What whole thing?"

"The thing you imagined! I'm not going to talk about it! And neither are you!"

"You're not the boss of me."

Honey looked disgusted. "You're acting like such a baby!"

"I can't take it," I said, sitting down on the bed. "I can't live with a vampire anymore."

"Will you stop that shit?" She threw her hairbrush on the floor. "Do you want to get locked up, like Mama did?"

"He's killing us. When are you going to wake up? Have you taken a look at your neck lately?"

"I told you. Bradley did it."

"Bradley didn't do that."

"How do you know? You weren't there." Honey's fury was exhausted. She began to cry. "The counselor won't believe you. They'll send you away."

"We can't stay here anymore," I said. "Uncle Toddy has to go or we go. That's it."

"You know they won't kick him out," she said, sobbing.

"Why not? Don't they care about their own children?"

"Nobody's going to believe you! You can't prove he's a vampire. It's just going to be your word against his."

"You can tell them too. They'll listen to you."

"Oh, great," Honey groaned. "I can see it now: 'Insurance Man's Family Goes Completely Insane.' Papa would die, he'd be so embarrassed."

"He'd rather we shut up and keep living with a vampire?"

"I don't know," she moaned. "Leave me alone."

"I've got proof. I've written it down in this book."

"What book?"

"My journal."

"Where is it? Let me see it."

"No," I said. "You wouldn't like it."

Honey tore at her hair. "Now they'll know you're crazy! They'll have proof in writing!"

"This whole family is nuts, haven't you noticed? Everybody goes around with bags over their heads. And if you pull off the bags, they say: 'Put that back!' Nobody wants to see what's happening!"

"Nothing's happening! It's all in your imagination."

"It's in your imagination too."

Honey's tears had dried up, and her eyes were cold. "If you go to the counselor, I'll never talk to you again. Do you hear what I'm saying? I mean it."

"We have to do this together! I'm trying to help you!"

But Honey wouldn't talk anymore.

After watching Nancy and Curtis Bradley drive away, I had started toward the administration building, which houses the counselor's office. But somehow I had arrived beside the pool. There was no one in it. A boy walked by and said, "Looking for the coach?"

"No," I said. I didn't know why I was there. The pool was the color of the sky. When I squinted my eyes, the two came together, no dividing line, no horizon.

I headed back the other way, toward the administration building. I looked at my watch. I was an hour late. Ms. Johnson had probably gone home.

I entered the building. It echoed with my footsteps. The heavy double doors crashed closed behind me. I was in a polished hallway lined with metal lockers. Most of the classrooms were open, deserted. A custodian pushing a broom disappeared around the corner. The door to Ms. Johnson's office was closed. But a light inside was shining through the frosted glass.

Before I could knock, Honey stepped out of the shadows between rows of lockers. I knew this would happen. I knew she would be here.

She looked so strange, so agitated. Maybe that's how she always looks; we're too close for me to see her clearly. The other day I was in the girls' bathroom and I looked in the mirror and it was full of faces, and I wasn't sure which one was me. For a second I wasn't sure. I know that sounds crazy.

"Don't go in there," Honey said. "I'm begging you. Please."

"Come with me," I said. "I need you."

"You promised not to tell."

"He said he'd kill Grammy."

"He never said he'd kill her! You're a goddamned liar! He never said that at all!" Honey hissed. "He said it would kill her if anything happened to the family.

Remember what happened when Mama got sick? Grammy got so sad she almost died."

"She's not going to die."

"This is all your fault! Just for once can you stop being selfish?"

"I'm not being selfish! Whose side are you on?"

"Mine," Honey said flatly, "and the family's."

"There is no family! There's just a bunch of people in a house!"

"That's a terrible thing to say! You're sick."

"I'm not going to kill them; I'm just going to tell the truth. It can't be worse than the way we're living."

"If you go in that room, I'll never talk to you again. You'll be all alone."

"I already am," I said.

I put my hand on the knob and pushed open the door. Ms. Johnson was standing behind her desk, wearing her coat, stuffing papers into a briefcase.

"Carolyn." She sighed. "I was just going home. You're very late."

"I know. I'm sorry. It's not important. We can talk some other time."

Her mouth was a straight line, and her eyes were tired. There was a smudge of ink on her chin.

"No, sit down, please."

"I can come back tomorrow."

"Really, this is fine," she said.

She sat down with her coat on. "I was looking through your file." She ransacked her desk but couldn't find it.

"I know what my grades are. They're not too great."

Ms. Johnson said, "That's an understatement, Carolyn. Your grade-point average has gone into the cellar."

The words sponged my brain clean. "I know," I said finally. "I can't concentrate lately." Why had I come here? If I didn't leave, Honey would hate me.

"There's obviously a problem. What do you think it might be?"

"I don't know," I said. "Maybe the weather."

"The weather?"

"I mean, it's springtime. I mean, the weather's so nice it's hard to think about school."

What was I saying? What had I wanted to tell her? I couldn't remember. My mouth was empty.

"Well, Carolyn, your grades started dropping months ago, so I don't think the weather's a big factor." She rocked in her chair, waiting for me to speak. "Carolyn," she said, "I'd like to help you, but I can't hold a gun to your head and make you talk."

No one can make me talk. You can torture me with knives. You can bleed me dry. I'll never tell.

"I know," I said, "I just feel kind of funny. I don't know what to say. I don't want to hog the conversation."

I looked around her office. It was crowded and messy. There were pictures of her children and husband on the walls, and an M&M package in the overflowing wastebasket. The plain kind, no nuts. My favorite.

"Look at me, Carolyn." Ms. Johnson leaned forward, her eyes on mine. She must've blinked when I blinked, because her gaze never faltered. "I know something's very wrong. It's written all over your face."

"My head, you mean."

"Yes." She smiled. "That's quite a hairstyle. Maybe I'll get mine cut like that too." She was trying to relax me. I didn't say anything. "You've got to help me, Carolyn. I know that you're articulate. I've read some of your writing. It's very good."

"It's easier to write things down than say them. I wonder why that is," I said. "I keep a journal."

"Really?" Ms. Johnson looked interested. "I always mean to do that, but I don't have the discipline. I do it for a while, then I forget."

"I do it all the time," I said. "I write things down."

"Have you written things down about your problem?"

"Problem?"

"The reason you're here. The reason you're failing in school."

"There are a couple of problems," I said. What were they? There were a couple of things I'd wanted to tell her.

"Can you talk about them now?"

"Maybe not," I said. Ms. Johnson looked at me and waited. "But maybe I could write them down."

"Well, that's an idea. Let's try that." She got out a pad of paper and a pen. "I'll ask you a question, then you write down the answer."

"What if I don't know the answer?"

"This isn't a test, Carolyn. Just write down what you're thinking. How does that sound?"

"Kind of dumb," I said.

"Let's try it and see."

"All right, if you want to."

Her face was so kind. I hated to write anything that would make her stop smiling. I moved closer to her desk and picked up the pen.

"Is there something wrong at home?" asked Ms. Johnson.

Yes, I wrote, and turned the pad so she could read it.

"Do you want to tell me what's wrong?" she asked.

I underlined the first *Yes* for my answer.

"Why can't you talk about it?"

I can, I wrote. *But I don't want to hear what I'd say.*

"Why not?"

Because, I wrote. *Bad things might happen.*

"What kind of bad things?"

I wrote: *I can't say.*

"Is the problem in your family?"

Yes.

"A family problem. Are you talking about Richie?"
She's tried to talk with him. He keeps his mouth shut,
unlike little Miss Blabbermouth. I'm writing, not telling.
Is that okay, Richie? Richie, please don't hate me.

No, not Richie.

"Your parents? Is the problem with your mother
or dad?"

Sort of. Not exactly.

"Your sister?"

No.

"Who else is there? Are you talking about your
grandparents?"

No, they're fine.

"Who are you talking about?"

I watched my hand form the letters, write the words.
My uncle.

"Your uncle? Does he live with you?"

Yes, I wrote. *Down the hall.*

"What's his name?"

His name is Uncle Toddy. But that's not what we call him.

"What who calls him?"

Me and my sister.

"What do you and your sister call him?"

"Don't tell!" Honey screamed at me. *"They'll send you
away!"*

"Carolyn, what do you and your sister call him?"

Uncle Vampire. I wrote the words again: *Uncle Vampire.* Once for Honey, once for me.

Ms. Johnson looked at the words, then at me. "Why do you call him that? What do you mean?"

He's a vampire. My printing had gotten very small, infant letters creeping across the page, tiny words hiding between the lines.

"How do you know he's a vampire?"

He drinks our blood. I unrolled my turtleneck and pointed to the fresh bruises on my throat. My heart was pounding. I heard metal doors clanging. Voices were chanting the Lord's Prayer, backward. The chanting got louder and louder.

"Carolyn, stay with me. You're drifting away. Do your parents know?"

Know what? I wrote. She looked surprised.

"What we were talking about. That your uncle's a vampire. Does he act like a vampire around your parents?"

No, I wrote. *Only with us.*

"Your sister and you. Does he attack Richie too?"

No. He's afraid of Richie. Richie knows. That's why he's going crazy.

"Richie or your uncle? Who's going crazy?"

Everybody, I wrote. *But Richie less. He wants to be blind, but he can see.*

"Have you told your parents that your uncle's a vampire?" Ms. Johnson's face was grave, her eyes impossible to read.

I tried to tell my father a long time ago, but he didn't

believe me. Or didn't want to believe me. I don't know. They're in a trance, I wrote.

"How long has your uncle been drinking your blood?" Ms. Johnson stared at the marks on my neck. I couldn't tell what she was thinking.

A long time. Ever since we were little. But now it's worse. He takes too much. He's killing us. I can't remember.

"Remember what?"

I cannot remember. What was I saying? I am all alone. No one can save me.

I looked up and saw fear on Ms. Johnson's face, before she could hide it. She was afraid. Of me. She had pushed back her chair. She thinks I'm crazy. *"See?"* Honey shrieked. *"I told you not to tell!"*

Then the expression on Ms. Johnson's face changed. I could see that she understood, that she believed me. I was so relieved I almost burst into tears, and I never cry now. I never cry.

She scooted her chair close, her knees pressing mine, then reached out and took my hands.

"Carolyn," she said. "Look at me. Your uncle's not a vampire, is he?"

I am spinning around, inside my mind. There's a crackling in my ears. Voices laughing and shrieking. *I'm not crazy!* Then I'm up on the ceiling, looking down, watching myself write: *I'M NOT CRAZY!*, scrawling the words across the paper.

Why don't I speak?

"I'm not saying you're crazy," Ms. Johnson says gently. "But you must tell me the truth. It's very important, Carolyn. Your uncle's not a vampire, is he?"

The chanting in my head is so loud I can't hear her. Her lips are moving. No sound comes out. You promised not to tell. I am suffocating. The dark wings of his cape are across my mouth.

No, I write. *He's not a vampire.*

I can't look in her eyes. I am so ashamed.

"Then why did you say that? Answer me, Carolyn."

Because, I finally write, *it's better to pretend. It's better than what he is.*

She lifts my chin and looks into my eyes. I am trapped inside them; there is no place to hide. She sees me.

"Carolyn, why would you make up a story like that? Tell me the truth. What's been happening? Why does he seem like a vampire to you? What has he done to you and your sister?"

Flames race toward me. The whole house is blazing. Fiery walls collapse around me. I crash through the glass that holds me in the burning room and plunge into space.

I say: "He fucks us."

Our Father, Who art in Heaven, hallowed be Thy name.

Don't say His name. You are an evil child. God doesn't love you anymore.

I did nothing wrong. I committed no crime. I'm telling you the truth.

Liar. He's a nice man and he loves you very much. Has he ever hurt you? He would never hurt you!

The voices scream. My ears are bleeding. I have fallen through a hole in the bottom of darkness, a drain through shadows into furred despair. Animals lunge at me, meat and teeth. Thy kingdom come, Thy will be done—

God can't help you. You are such a dirty girl. You will burn in hell for the things you are saying, for the harm you have done your family.

My uncle surrounds me. He fills the sky. I try to scream; he shrouds my mouth. I'm not crazy. I've got proof. I hid the journal under my bed. Grammy, won't you give me my daily bread? And teach me to forgive those who trespass against me—

Grammy, he has hurt me so badly.

He said he loved me, but he never did. He ate up my love and betrayed me. I felt like I was dying, but he kept me alive, and murdered me again and again and again.

Lead us not into temptation but deliver us from evil—

The voices in my head are shouting: Kill her. They are saying I killed Grammy. Grammy's dead. She is lying at my feet. My shoes are soaked with blood. She will never speak to me again.

"Carolyn, look at me."

Ms. Johnson shakes my shoulders. Mice squeak and chatter, gnawing through the walls.

"Stay with me, Carolyn. It will be all right, I promise. You're breathing too fast. Take it easy."

My lungs are burning. I have forgotten how to breathe. I rest my head on my knees.

"Listen to me, Carolyn. Everything will be all right. I know this is very difficult. But we're going to work it out. Can you hear me, Carolyn?"

"Yes," I gasp. My chest is cracking. I am having a heart attack. He has attacked my heart.

"You're saying that your uncle sexually abused you and your sister."

I don't have the breath to speak. I nod my head.

She strokes my hair. "I'm so sorry, Carolyn. I'm so very, very sorry." Her voice is a whisper. "How long has this been going on?"

My uncle drowns her out. He shouts into my mouth: *"Don't tell!"*

"Forever. I don't know. Since we were little."

Ms. Johnson's head droops, as if too heavy for her neck. I will die if I see disgust on her face, if I see that she despises me. Evil. Whore.

Her face is soft with pity. She pats my back.

"You pretended he was a vampire because the truth was worse. The reality was too awful. Am I understanding you, Carolyn?"

Yes. I nod.

"What a brave little girl you must have been. How terrible it was for you. Did your sister think he was a vampire too?"

"At first she did, but then she started pretending that nothing was wrong. She couldn't face it. I mean, we just—he told us not to tell! He said that something bad would happen!"

"Calm down, sweetie. It's all right." Her arms enclose

me. "He's never going to hurt you again. When we're done here today, I'm going to call the police."

"No, you can't! My mother, my father—" I can picture the looks on their faces. Who will they be angry at? Him or me?

"Of course they'll want to know. Don't you think they'll want to help you?"

I really don't know the answer.

"I'm required by law to report this, Carolyn. The police will do an investigation and arrest him. In the meantime, we need to get you and your sister out of that house. Has he hurt Richie too? Can you hear me, Carolyn?"

You'll have to go away. They'll send you away. You'll never see your Grammy again. Your Grammy will die. Your Grammy will hate you.

"Has he molested Richie too? Please answer me, Carolyn."

The worst wounds aren't the ones that can be seen; they scar your heart and cripple your brain.

"I don't think he's ever touched him. But Richie feels crazy because he can't stop it, he can't do anything. Richie won't look in my eyes anymore. He's ashamed of me. He's ashamed of himself." My tongue fills my throat. I can barely speak.

"What about your sister? Will she talk about this?"

"No. She says it's all in my head. She says I'm crazy, I'm making it up. She knows what's true, but she's so scared. She gets so scared she won't even wake up, and I'm the one that has to deal with everything, I'm the one who has to face it."

"I thought she was away at school."

"Who?"

"Margaret."

"I'm not talking about Maggie. I'm talking about Honey. She's scared we're going to get in trouble. She didn't want me to talk to you. She wants me to keep pretending everything's fine, but I can't. I told her we have to do something right now or I really will go crazy. Or maybe I'll die. Sometimes I want to, just to get away. I mean, I want to live. But not in hell. I try to help her, but she won't listen!"

Ms. Johnson looks like she's going to cry. I want to assure her that I'm okay. No big deal; it's just my life. You can't make it stop and you can't escape. You don't have a choice; you're just a kid.

"It's not that bad," I say, to comfort her. "Really."

Her face is so sad. She takes my hands.

"Honey," she says, "you don't have another sister."

"I know," I say. "That's the other problem."

I can't remember when it started. When I was little. My sister Honey was a game that I played, a favorite blanky that I carried. She kept me warm.

Nancy's brother said that everybody had a twin, that somewhere in the world there was someone just like you. So I pretended that my twin lived in the mirror. She was just like me but left-handed.

Maggie was busy with her friends and school, and Richie didn't want me around. Well, he didn't mind, but his friends teased him, so when I followed him, he said, "Beat it, kid."

One day I said to the girl in the mirror: "I wish you could come out and play with me." And she said, "Okay," and then she did.

I was glad to have her with me. She came in handy, like when they sent me to my room without supper. I always felt sad, but they never asked why. They thought I acted moody on purpose, to bug them. They liked Honey better. She always tried to please them. She tried to get me to please them too, but sometimes I couldn't figure out what they wanted.

They'd be saying two different things at once. Like: "Don't be rude. Give your uncle a kiss." And: "Yes, you're entitled to your own opinion, but do what I tell you, do you hear me?"

They sent me to my room and I cried for Grammy, but she was at her house and couldn't hear me. No one could hear me; my face was pressed down into the pillow.

Honey heard me. She said, "Don't be sad. I'll fix things so no one will be mad at you."

She went downstairs and kissed his cheek and everybody liked her, she was such a good girl. She knew what to say to make them happy.

It worked out well, the two of us together. My life was too much for one person to cope with.

My uncle hurt Honey, but she cried, she got scared. She'd run away and hide in the piano. Later, I'd tell her what had happened and she didn't remember, and she didn't want to know. At first that was okay, but then it didn't seem fair that she got to go away and I had to stay there. He scared me too. Why did I have to be the brave one? So then I went away, far inside my mind, where my uncle couldn't reach me. I was at the beach and the sun was warm and Grammy was hugging me and singing a song, and saying, "Honey, you're my darling girl."

The whole time, I told myself: This is not happening.

What wasn't happening? I'd forget.

This journal was the place where I put the ugly words. Sometimes I didn't even notice I was writing.

Later, I would find the words and wonder: Where did this come from? Did Honey write this?

Deep down, I always knew that he wasn't a vampire.

But the truth about my uncle was too awful to bear. He was a parasite, sucking the blood out of babies. He was a cannibal, feasting on his family.

"Look at me," he'd say. "Open your eyes and look."

Deep down, I always knew that Honey wasn't real.

But she was the only one who understood me, who knew what my life was truly like, who shared the darkness of my heart.

Without her, I would have been so lonely.

I have been living with Maggie and Michael for several months. When I wake up crying in the night, Maggie comforts me. She holds my hand while I fall asleep.

We live in a small house across from a park. I watch the children riding on the swings, the little girls climbing into the sky.

I see a psychologist three times a week.

I'm out of school, on independent study.

My uncle is in jail. He's going to prison. I never have to see him again.

He writes me letters that I won't read, telling me he's sorry and begging forgiveness.

He believes that he didn't really hurt me.

Maggie says: "Why didn't you tell me? I wouldn't have thought you were crazy."

I tell her that I wish she had told me too. I understand why she didn't. She was little; she told Papa that Uncle Toddy tickled her. Oh, he's just playing, Papa said. But Uncle Toddy never bothered her again.

She'd always assumed that the problem was solved. I guess Papa did too.

* * *

I was ashamed to tell anyone what he was doing to me. I thought I must be very bad to make such bad things happen. If they knew the real me, people would hate me. No one would love me. That's what I thought.

My therapist says that disguising my uncle as a vampire and inventing Honey were "coping mechanisms," defenses that enabled me to survive in an unpredictable and profoundly dysfunctional situation.

Now it's time to face reality.

Sometimes it's ugly. He said he'd kill Grammy. That the truth would kill Grammy.

It hasn't. But she cries on the phone. It was very hard to leave her. I'm going back to see her and Grampa this summer.

I haven't spoken to my parents in weeks.

I am so angry at them. At first they acted sorry for me; then they tried to convince me that I was exaggerating. Things weren't as bad as I'd imagined. They wanted Honey back.

"Honey," they said, when the cops came, "you don't mean that. Honey, you don't know what you're saying."

"Yes, I do," I said. Honey was gone.

*   *   *

Today I got a letter from Bradley Curtis. He said he hopes I'm doing fine. He said he's looking forward to seeing me this summer.

He and Nancy think I'll be back at school with them in the fall. But my life there seems like it took place on another planet.

Therapy is hard. It's like digging through mud, looking for bones, or weapons, or treasures. At first my therapist used the word *molest*.

"He didn't molest me; he abused me," I said. "Molest sounds like something Chihuahuas do to your legs. Abuse is the dogs of hell."

When did it start? How young was I? I try to remember what I'd rather forget. The splinter must come out, but it will hurt. I remember bits and pieces. Pictures drop into my mind. I am floating in water, my hair was in the water, he's pulling at my hair. I'm scared, I'm drowning, he gathers me up, the lights go out.

Please, don't ask me any more.

I will tell you, when I'm stronger.

Richie drove me to the airport and put me on the plane for Boston. He gave me a long hug before he let me go.

He said, "I'm so sorry."

"It's not your fault, Rich."

"I tried to tell the folks. They never listened. They don't listen to a damn thing I say. I should've done something. I didn't know what to do."

"I didn't either. We were just kids."

"Yeah," Richie said, "but now we're not."

He doesn't live at home anymore.

I'm also in group therapy, with a bunch of other kids, girls and boys, some younger than me, some older. They were abused by their fathers, brothers, mothers, strangers. We share our histories and our hurts.

I've been doing a lot of reading too. Vampires like my uncle are as common as termites, infesting even the best homes. Their victims number in the millions. Often, the children don't remember what happened. The shock and the pain and the betrayal are too great. So the children lock a door against the memories and grow up.

But the memories keep knocking at the locked door.

And the knocking drives them crazy.

No one came to my rescue. I saved myself. I have begun to heal. This book is a scar. Don't get me wrong; I don't wake up whistling.

But I wake up. It's a start.

I have to work hard to stay in the present, to resist the temptation to pretend, to tell myself that it couldn't have happened.

It shouldn't have happened. But it did.

I wrote it all down here where everyone can see it, pinned the words on the page so they can't get away, and I have to look at the truth and face it. Face it, Carolyn. Don't be afraid. The night has passed. The sun is bright.

It's hard to get rid of vampires. You have to drag them into the light.

If you are being physically, sexually, or emotionally abused, tell someone you trust. Tell a teacher, a counselor, your minister, a relative; tell any adult who will get you the help you deserve and need.

You may need to tell more than one person before you find someone who will listen. Keep telling until you find someone who will help you.

Your local police can help. So can the Child Protective Agency in your area. Call information and ask the operator for the phone numbers.

You may also call Childhelp USA/IOF, the National Child Abuse Hot Line, toll-free, twenty-four hours a day, at 1-800-422-4453. If they're busy, you might be asked to wait for a few minutes. Hold on, or call back. The counselors there will help you.

Don't be afraid. And don't give up.